Rafe's kiss deepened, becoming more demanding as he felt her response. 'Darling—darling——' His voice was anguished as he lifted her in his arms and carried her into the bedroom and lowered her on to the big bed. 'Can we—please——?' he pleaded.

From some remote part of Sara's mind came the message, clear as a bell. *You can't—you mustn't—it's all wrong. It isn't you he wants, it's another woman.*

*Another book you will enjoy
by MARJORIE LEWTY*

A KISS IS STILL A KISS

James Warrington came into Victoria's life when she needed help desperately and had no one to turn to. It was natural that she should be grateful to him—but where did the boundary lie between gratitude and love?

MAN-TRAP

BY

MARJORIE LEWTY

MILLS & BOON LIMITED
ETON HOUSE   18-24 PARADISE ROAD
RICHMOND   SURREY   TW9 1SR

All the characters in this book have no existence outside the imagination of the Author, and have no relation whatsoever to anyone bearing the same name or names. They are not even distantly inspired by any individual known or unknown to the Author, and all the incidents are pure invention.

All Rights Reserved. The text of this publication or any part thereof may not be reproduced or transmitted in any form or by any means, electronic or mechanical, including photocopying, recording, storage in an information retrieval system, or otherwise, without the written permission of the publisher.

MILLS & BOON and Rose Device is registered in U.S. Patent and Trademark Office.

First published in Great Britain 1990 by Mills & Boon Limited

© Marjorie Lewty 1990

Australian copyright 1990

ISBN 0 263 12385 5

Set in Times 11 on 12 pt. 07–9003–51192

Typeset in Great Britain by JCL Graphics, Bristol

Made and Printed in Great Britain

CHAPTER ONE

SARA felt her skin prickle the moment he walked into the design office. It was as if a hungry predator had appeared suddenly among a peaceful herd of grazing cattle. He stood quite still in the doorway, tall, dark, impressive, wearing a silver-grey suit, white shirt and striped tie. A man exuding authority from every inch of his long, hard-muscled body.

A low murmur of 'Good morning, sir' floated on the air, which he acknowledged with a brief nod of his dark head. Brooding, near-black eyes passed cursorily over the double row of drawing-boards—nine young men, suddenly very busily engaged with architectural plans and elevations, working drawings, scale measurements—and came to rest on the bright flame of Sara's head in her corner of the long office.

He strode across and stopped before her drawing-table. 'Who are you?' he rapped out.

Clear green eyes lifted artlessly to his. 'Sara Bennett,' Sara said, and—because she wasn't prepared to accept meekly the gratuitous rudeness of the man's tone, whoever he might be—she added, 'Who are you?'

A flicker of outraged anger showed in the dark eyes. The straight mouth firmed dangerously. 'The name's Jordan.'

'Oh yes, of course,' Sara gave him her wide, candid smile. 'Mr Jordan.' She stood up and held out her hand. 'You've been in France, haven't you? I only started here last week. How do you do, Mr Jordan.'

She was aware of heads turning, of eyes fixed on the small tableau in her corner of the room. The juniors and pupils in the design office seemed to be holding their communal breath.

For a moment she thought he was going to ignore the hand she held out. Then, briefly, he enclosed it in his own. Sara almost gasped. It was as if she had touched a live electric wire. Heavens, the man was lethal—why hadn't anyone warned her? But of course the other occupants of the design office were all male—indubitably male, if their reaction to *her* was anything to go by.

'Miss Bennett,' the newcomer acknowledged frostily. He nodded towards the immaculate and complicated plan drawing on her desk. 'Don't let me interrupt your work.' He strode towards the inner office and disappeared inside.

The booming voice of the senior partner drifted out. 'Rafe, you're back. Good lad. Had a successful trip?'

An unintelligible growl in reply. Sara had excellent hearing and the next words reached her quite clearly in her corner by the door to the inner office. 'Dad, why the hell did you have to replace young Carpenter with a *girl*? And a girl like that, too. We've managed to keep women out of the design office up to now.'

A chuckle from Mr Jordan Senior came floating out. He said something in an amused tone, but Sara didn't catch the words. Then the door was closed with a sharp click as if pushed by an impatient foot.

Sara sat back in her chair and let out her breath. Well, that was nice, wasn't it? A charming reception! Not, 'How do you do, Miss Bennett, welcome to the firm.' Or, 'I hope you'll be happy among us.' Oh, no, merely, 'Don't let me interrupt your work,' accompanied by a glower. And his words to his father! What sort of a man was the junior partner? Not a woman-hater, surely? Not with that lean, dynamic body and those dark, slumbrous eyes. He breathed sexuality without even trying.

Bob Stratton wandered over, carrying a rolled sheet of tracing paper to the large copier at the side of the office. He paused on the way to grin cheerfully at Sara. 'Fallen foul of our local paper tiger already, have you? It had to happen, of course.'

Sara looked up at him, puzzled. 'Why, for goodness'sake? He's never seen me before.'

Bob glanced at the clock on the wall. 'Lunchtime for you and me,' he said. 'Wait till I've run this copy through and then come out and sample the new McDonald's with me and I'll put you wise.'

So far Sara had politely evaded invitations from the young men in the department. She had to get to know them all and find her feet first. But this offer was too tempting to refuse. Mr Rafe Jordan, junior partner and head of the design department, was back in the office, making it plain that he didn't want her there, and she had to know what sort of a fight she had on her hands. 'I'll take you up on that, Bob,' she said. 'See you downstairs in a few minutes.' She picked up her handbag and made for the cloakroom on the floor below.

In the office of the senior partner, the senior partner's son was sprawled in the visitor's chair scowling across the vast oak desk at his illustrious parent, who was regarding him with an amused and tolerant expression on his still handsome face.

The Jordans, father and son, were quite extraordinarily alike. Donald Jordan, dark and magnificently fit at fifty-six, still caused feminine hearts to flutter. His son Rafe was equally dark, even more fit, but his eyes were not quizzical and tolerant like his father's. They were moody and disdainful and glared out at the world with a stern glitter in their black depths that did not invite a closer contact.

At the moment dark brows were drawn down over them. 'I'll never get any decent work out of those lads out there with a red-haired, green-eyed chit like that one flaunting herself all over the office.'

'Rubbish.' His father's tone was crisp. 'I haven't noticed any flaunting going on. In point of fact, the standard of work has improved quite dramatically since Sara arrived. Having a pretty girl in the office puts a zip in the atmosphere. Wakens things up, keeps the boys on their toes.'

'I bet it does,' Rafe said sourly.

Donald Jordan looked faintly irritated. 'Give the girl a chance, Rafe. She's a nice girl—quiet, highly competent. She came to me through Tom Field, who gave her the very highest recommendation. She's been with Field's in Winchester ever since she qualified and only wanted to move to London for—personal reasons.'

'Personal reasons!' A sneer twisted Rafe Jordan's handsome mouth. 'Let me guess—involving a man?'

His father gave him a bland look. 'Indeed so. Following the death of her father and selling up the home.'

'Oh!' His son had the grace to look faintly deflated. 'Oh, well, I suppose I'll have to put up with her in my department for the time being. She's on some sort of trial, is she?'

'A month, either side. But I don't anticipate the option being taken up,' his father said, and there was a warning note in his voice.

He got up and came round the desk to put a large, firm hand on his son's shoulder. 'Get rid of that chip, Rafe. You'll find the right girl for you one of these days.'

'I wouldn't bet on it,' Rafe said gloomily. He looked up into the older man's face and added quickly, 'You were lucky, Dad.' The hardness had left his voice, the dark eyes were suddenly tender. 'Mum was one in a million.'

'I know,' Donald Jordan said quietly. He turned away and went back to his chair across the desk. 'Now,' he said very briskly, 'tell me all about your French trip.'

Jordan's London office was as superbly equipped as any of the prestigious residences the firm designed for rich clients. In the deep-carpeted ladies' room on the second floor Sara washed her hands at a rose-pink ceramic basin and thought dismally that it had been too good to last, landing a job with a top firm of architects like Jordan's, and enjoying the work, and fitting in so well. Up to now. There was bound to be a catch in it somewhere, a fly in the ointment. Some fly!

And what did he mean by 'a girl like that', for heaven's sake? She stared at her reflection in the pink-tinted mirror above the wash basin. She hadn't got two heads; she wasn't even sprouting devil's horns. She was a perfectly ordinary young woman with a pleasant enough face, hair frankly red—although Daddy, an artist, had always called it

Titian—a rather too wide mouth, and eyes the green of a Perrier-water bottle. So what was he objecting to?

As if she cared! His father seemed to like her, and his father was head of the firm, not Mr Macho Rafe. Sara grinned at herself and released her hair from its restraining ribbon bow. She couldn't bear to have strands hanging forward when she was bending over her drawing-table. Also, she planned her appearance to be strictly businesslike in the office. It was a nice balance. She might be working in a profession that was still mostly a masculine preserve, but that didn't mean that she need hide her femininity. Neither need she emphasise it.

Out of the office she liked to wear her hair loose. It gave her the feeling of freedom and independence she valued. She leaned towards the tinted mirror, combing out the silky dark red mass until it clung round her ears and fell in a nice curve into her neck. She emphasised her lips with a new cinnamon-coloured lipstick and blotted them carefully. She took a white linen jacket from her locker, pulled it on over the straight-fitting, black-and-white patterned dress, which covered her knees modestly, and went to join Bob Stratton downstairs.

He was waiting for her, chatting to the commissionaire in his box beside the lift. Bob Stratton was the most senior of the young men in the design department—in fact, very nearly a fully-fledged architect at twenty-six or seven. Well over six feet tall and painfully thin, with floppy fairish hair, he already had a slight stoop from years of bending over a drawing-table. He always looked to Sara like a boy who had, as her grandmother would have said, overgrown his strength. He came eagerly towards the lift as the gate clanged, beaming broadly. 'You look great with your hair loose,' he greeted Sara, 'McDonald's, here we come!' He winked at the commissionaire, who raised one thumb behind Sara's back.

'This is nice,' said Bob, cosily linking an arm with Sara's as they crossed the marble-floored lobby. 'Do I have to thank our Rafe for the honour of escorting you to lunch?'

'Not entirely,' Sara assured him. She had an idea that Bob wasn't as confident as he appeared and she wouldn't want to hurt his feelings. 'But I must admit I'm curious about why he gave me the glacial treatment.'

Bob waited until they were sitting in the window of the McDonald's, with healthy-looking hamburgers and containers of Coke before them on the yellow-topped table. Then he said, 'Trouble with Rafe Jordan is, he hasn't any time for nice girls, and he must have seen at a glance that you come into that category, Sara.'

Green eyes opened wide in puzzlement. 'Really?'

'Yes, really. A bloke can tell at a glance, you know.' Bob pursed his lips and nodded, very worldly-wise.

'Go on,' smiled Sara. 'This is interesting. And why hasn't Mr Jordan any time for nice girls—like me?' she added, biting into her hamburger.

'He's divorced, poor devil. Plays havoc with your approach to women. Seen it happen lots of times—my own brother couldn't look at a decent girl for ages after his divorce. Only went for the floozies!'

Sara nodded slowly. 'I—see.' She was trying to remember the time, all those years ago, when her mother had walked out on her father, and what it did to him. She hadn't noticed any floozies about then. But of course Daddy was different—he was an artist, and artists had their own individual way of responding to things. She did remember that for a long time afterwards he could hardly be dragged away from his studio. And in the weeks before he died, when she came closer to him than ever before, he confided, 'Don't think I've been lonely, Sara. I know now it was the best thing that could have happened when you mother left. I must have been a rotten husband. Artists usually are.'

She had wanted to fling her arms round his neck in a tempest of love and loyalty and say, 'You couldn't be a rotten anything, and you're a wonderful father.' Of course she hadn't, because she knew a display of emotion would have embarrassed him. But she'd never loved him more than she did at that moment—only a few months ago.

'Oh, well,' she said now, wrenching her mind back from that unhappy time, 'perhaps that explains things. Do you think if I let my hair loose in the office and put a bit more stuff on my face I'd be welcomed to the team by our chief?'

Bob guffawed loudly. 'You couldn't look like a floozie if you tried, Sara. And Rafe Jordan isn't worth the effort, anyway. Look, how about coming to see a film with me tonight?' His thin face had pinkened slightly.

Sara shook her head reluctantly. 'Thanks a lot, Bob, but I've got a date already. Sorry.' The 'date' was with a pot of paint and a paintbrush; she had started on the much needed redecoration of her flatlet.

'Yes, of course,' Bob said hastily. 'Oh, well, some other time, then.'

She smiled and nodded, and after that they began to talk shop about the design of a new country house the firm was working on for a high-up managing director in the City. Bob was brilliant at his job and Sara listened intently, always ready to pick up any detail that would add to her knowledge of her chosen profession. One day she was going to be a real architect, seeing buildings take shape to her own design. It would be a marvellous thrill. Even though she worked for years and years it would be worth it in the end.

Once launched on his own subject Bob was all confidence. He talked well, and it wasn't until Sara looked at her watch and gasped, 'Golly, we're going to be late getting back!' that he flushed and said, 'You should have stopped me.'

'Certainly not,' Sara said, standing up. 'I'd much rather listen to you than go back to the office.' Which wasn't entirely true, but Bob's grin of pleasure excused the little white lie.

They hurried along the maze of roads at the back of Oxford Street. In early August, London was hot, and crowded with tourists, and Sara was breathing quite fast when they finally arrived back at the office—a modern white building sandwiched between two old, grimy ones. It had an impressive entrance, and a discreet bronze plate beside the front door which announced. 'Donald E. Jordan FRIBA, Rafe Jordan ARIBA, Architects'.

Bob was all for dashing up the stairs, but Sara panted, 'Let's wait for the lift, I'm creased!'

Then she wished she hadn't. For the gate of the descending lift opened to emit Mr Rafe Jordan, carrying a black leather portfolio, obviously on his way to visit a client. He paused momentarily, staring from Sara's gently heaving bosom and the thick fall of silky red hair hanging loose around her face to Bob's flushed cheeks. Then he looked pointedly at his wristwatch and walked past them in silence.

'Bastard!' Bob muttered under his breath, and pulled the lift gate open again with an angry swish. 'We're not more than five minutes late.' He waited for Sara to get in the lift and pressed the button with a jab of a long finger.

Sara didn't reply. She was putting her own construction on Rafe Jordan's cold, disapproving glare. He didn't like her, he didn't want her in his department and he would take every opportunity to ... to ... She went cold suddenly. To get rid of her? Or make it impossible for her to stay?

Sara felt slightly on edge for the rest of the afternoon, but the reason for the fluttering in her stomach every time the office door opened did not put in an appearance again, for which she was truly thankful.

It would take a little time, she told herself later, as she climbed the long flight of stairs to her tiny flatlet on the top floor of an old house in Bayswater, to get used to having someone around who struck a discordant note in what had been, up to now, a very happy working environment. But she *would* get used to it, she was determined on that. She wasn't giving up this opportunity; she'd never have a better one to get ahead in her chosen profession. Do your worst, Mr Rafe Jordan, I'm here to stay, she vowed as she put her key in the lock of the green-painted front door.

She loved her flatlet, tiny though it was. It represented the beginning of a whole new way of life.

She had adored her artist father, and after he died the thought of staying on alone in the cottage they had shared in Hampshire was quite unbearable. For a while she had rented a flat in Winchester and gone on working for Tom Field, but restlessness had nagged at her and finally she had taken her problem to the understanding Tom, who had suggested that he might be able to fix up a job for her with a firm in London. 'Donald Jordan is right at the top of the profession,' he'd said. 'If he has a vacancy it would be just the thing for you, Sara, sorry though I would be to lose you.'

Sara was sorry too; she had worked with the amiable Mr Field for two years—since she left university. But the scope of his work was fairly narrow—mostly renovations and extensions of existing houses. At Jordan's she was already working on large, exciting projects, and there were more in the pipeline. She'd been right to start a new life, she thought, as she moved about the little flat, grilling ham and heating baked beans for her supper. No one—certainly not Rafe Jordan—was going to spoil it for her. Having made that resolution, she sat down to enjoy her supper and plan her working schedule for the painting of her bedroom later on in the evening.

For the following week the design department saw little of Rafe Jordan and went on happily with its work. Then, on Friday afternoon, when they were packing up for the weekend, he came into the office with a large envelope in his hand. 'Take a look at these, all of you,' he invited.

Sara noticed that his glance had slid away from her very quickly, but she joined the others as they gathered round the side table on which he was spreading out a selection of photographs.

'This is something a bit different—and interesting,' he said. 'A commission to build a gallery—a small private gallery to house a collection belonging to Alain Savin. He's the owner of a large château in France, some kilometres from Paris. He and his wife turned the château into a hotel—a very exclusive hotel—several years ago. His wife was English and the work of reconstruction and extension was done by our firm through a connection of hers. It was probably before most of you started here—*you* may remember, Bob.'

Bob Stratton nodded. 'I went over there once. A super place—all among the trees, with a lake——'

'Yes,' Rafe cut him off briskly. 'Well, this is the gen. Alain Savin's wife, who, with Alain himself, was a dedicated collector of all sorts of things—pictures, costumes, ethnic items, Oriental bits and pieces—died a short time ago. He plans to build this small gallery where he can keep their collection together in one place. It will be in the grounds of the hotel, but well away from the hotel itself and its surroundings. These pictures will give you an idea of the locale.' He spread the photographs out on the table.

Sara peered round Bob Stratton's lanky body to see the glossy colour pictures, but she could only get a glimpse of low, feathery trees. There seemed to be a lake in the background and beside the lake, in the near distance, a kind of gazebo or summer-house.

She craned her neck to get a better view. What a beautiful place, and what a nice man this Alain Savin must be to build a gallery specially for his dead wife's collection. She swallowed a sigh. He must have loved her very much. Perhaps he meant to go to the gallery alone as if it were a kind of shrine, a memory of their love. They would have bought some of the pieces in the collection when they had travelled together . . .

She was jerked out of these sentimental thoughts by Rafe Jordan's deep, slightly abrasive voice, saying, 'I've already given Alain my own somewhat vague suggestions—there wasn't time to come up with anything very definite when I was there with him. What I would like is drawings from some of you to send along, so that he can have a selection to choose from. Nothing finished, not even schematic designs, more in the nature of artists' impressions, only roughly to scale. Get the idea?'

Sara looked round the faces of the assembled group, most of which seemed to be expressing dutiful acquiescence rather than wild enthusiasm. In her own mind something was stirring very strongly. This would be a marvellous project to work on—already she had the beginning of an idea——

Rafe Jordan was speaking again, and she dragged her attention back to what he was saying. ' . . . and now for the bad news. I'm afraid you'd have to do it in your own time. We can't afford to let it cut into the work on the Ferguson plans. Probably some of you wouldn't be interested, but I'd very much like to see drawings from you, Bob . . . and Richard . . .' He looked round the group in front of him. 'And you, Frank?' The dark eyes passed over Sara and slid away quickly. 'Right, I'll leave it with you, then. I'll want the drawings in a week from today at the latest.'

Sara wanted to get this straight from the start. 'Is it all right for me to submit a drawing, Mr Jordan?' She spoke clearly from her place at the back of the group.

Dark eyes turned towards her without really looking at her. 'Oh, I don't think so, Miss Bennett. Your experience would hardly warrant . . .' he began dismissively. Then a voice from behind them broke in.

'Of course you may, Sara. Excellent practice for you.'

Everyone looked round. Donald Jordan was standing in the doorway of his private office, smiling broadly at Sara. Then he turned his benevolent gaze on his son. 'I think that's only fair, don't you, Rafe?'

Sara flicked a momentary glance at Rafe and saw something like fury in his dark eyes. But his voice was even and controlled as he said, 'Very well, Miss Bennett, if you think you have the necessary talent for work like this, go ahead.'

She smiled composedly enough, but there was a glint of battle in the sparkly green eyes as she said, 'Oh, I believe I have, Mr Jordan. I'll do my best.'

And for a week she worked in the evenings in her little flat, the decoration postponed. She had managed to acquire from Bob one of the photographs of the grounds of the French château, and she roughed out one idea after another, sometimes pausing for thought, sometimes allowing her pencil to skim across the paper, scribbling down some detail before the visualisation of it faded.

She thought often of her father as she worked. How interested he would have been in this assignment, and how proud he would have been that she should have been chosen to send in a drawing. Chosen! That was hardly the right word. Rafe Jordan certainly hadn't chosen her, in fact he'd been all set to discourage her from competing. She didn't dwell on that too often: the memory of those dismissive black eyes sweeping over her as if he would like to sweep her bodily out of the building was inclined to put her off her work.

Sometimes, when an idea temporarily eluded her, she almost gave up the whole thing. Even if her finished drawing deserved to succeed, that man would manage to discredit it. Then she seemed to hear her father's voice say, 'Get on with it, girl. Don't let anyone put you off, you're doing fine.' And she set to work again.

There was a good deal of talk in the office about the progress of the drawings. Four hopefuls, including Sara, had admitted starting the project and two of them were making very heavy weather of it. Frank, who fancied himself as the answer to every female's prayer, complained that it interfered with his love-life. Richard moaned, 'It's like being back at school. Bloody homework!' Bob Stratton was working on the project rather secretively, but he had a smug look on his long, thin face which suggested he was pleased with his efforts.

When the day came to turn in the drawings Sara tried to feel hopeful. 'How's it gone?' Bob wanted to know, when work for the day was over and they met in the little annexe that housed the coffee machine and a couple of plan chests. 'Satisfied with your artistic efforts?'

'Is one ever?' Sara pulled a face, although she thought from Bob's expression that he might be the exception to the rule. 'You?'

He pressed the button that delivered coffee into his plastic mug. 'Tolerably satisfied. But you never know, especially dealing with foreigners; they don't see things the way we do. This Savin fellow—I met him once, years ago when we were doing work on the hotel—he struck me as being a bit over the top. You know, the way they wave their hands about when they're talking. I can't stick that type myself.'

Sara grinned. 'If your drawing's accepted you'll think differently about Monsieur Savin, won't you?'

Bob grinned. 'The price we have to pay for success! But it hasn't been accepted yet,' he added quickly. 'Maybe you'll top the list yourself.'

'I'll be so lucky,' Sara grimaced. How tactful they were both being, and they were both as nervous as kittens. 'Come on, let's deliver our efforts to the big boss.'

Ten minutes later the four juniors were assembled in the office of the senior partner. Donald Jordan was sitting behind his big desk and his son was standing beside him, one hand on the back of his father's chair. Sara was uncomfortably reminded of the times she went for interviews before she was finally accepted by Tom Field. It was absurd, but her mouth was dry and her hand that held her drawing-roll was clammy. It would have been so much better if Rafe Jordan hadn't been there; just glancing at the tall, formidable figure made her inside squeeze up. His dark head was bent over the desk, where Frank had unrolled his drawing for inspection. Sara's eyes were drawn unwillingly to the thick, dark thatch of hair. A bit on the long side perhaps, but she had to admit that it suited his style, gave him that touch of—what was it?—blunt directness allied to a certain artistic gift—which he cultivated.

Whenever he had had occasion to speak to her in the office in these last couple of weeks he hadn't troubled to be courteous, let alone pleasant. Directions were as brief as they could be and delivered with all the finesse of a sergeant-major. Sara didn't let it trouble her— much. She got on with her work and told herself that sooner or later he would get used to seeing her around and decide he might as well treat her as one of the team. One plus was that he hadn't had occasion to find fault with her work.

Frank's drawing had been examined, Richard's too. The two partners were poring over Bob's work now. Sara couldn't resist a peep at the drawing that he had obviously taken such care over, and bit her lip. If this was what was wanted, then she might as well tear up her own effort here and now. Bob's drawing was hardly an artist's impression. It was a scale plan in which he had managed cleverly to suggest the appearance of the finished building. The stone was colour-washed brown, the surrounding trees green, a hint of blue in the background that was the edge of the lake. All done with Bob's impeccable neatness and attention to detail.

'Hm, yes.' Donald Jordan nodded approvingly. 'Very nicely set out, Bob. Does you credit, don't you think, Rafe?'

'Excellent,' Rafe agreed, smiling.

Sara hadn't seen Rafe Jordan smile before and it gave her quite a shock. His whole face looked different, younger, more human. If the word hadn't been so inappropriate to describe him she might have thought he looked—kind.

Then the smile disappeared abruptly as he turned his eyes in Sara's direction with his rather hateful way of looking at her without looking. At least that was how it seemed; it was a trick, she realised. He always looked at a spot between her eyes instead of looking straight into them. 'OK, Miss Bennett, let's see the masterpiece you've come up with,' he drawled.

I hate him, Sara thought, spreading her work out on

the desk, weighting each side with paper weights to stop it rolling itself up again. I just can't bear the man, he's a pig!

She couldn't watch as the two partners examined her drawing. She looked out of the window over their heads at the London skyline. It had been one of those hot, humid summer days and now, at last, fat drops of rain were slowly splashing against the window and a rumble of thunder sounded in the distance. The sound reverberated in Sara's head and for a moment she felt almost faint. She really must pull herself together and not get so worked up. It wouldn't be the end of the world if they turned her work down flat. It would mean, though, that the abominable Rafe had scored heavily in his attempt to discredit her in his father's eyes.

'Well,' said the senior partner at last. 'It's certainly—different.'

His son appeared to be at a loss for words for a few moments. Then he said, with a studied politeness that was almost an insult, 'Perhaps you'd like to give us a few words of explanation of this——' he touched the drawing with one long, brown finger '— this work of art.'

Sara drew in a deep breath. 'Certainly, Mr Jordan. And may I remind you that what you asked for was an artist's impression? I took it that this was the sort of thing you wanted.'

Donald Jordan was still staring down at Sara's drawing. 'Yes,' he said slowly. 'Interesting. It certainly has something . . .'

Sara could have kissed him. Ignoring his son completely, she came round the desk and stood beside the senior partner. Eagerly she explained her drawing, and, once she had begun, her nervousness suddenly disappeared.

Picking up a gold pencil from the desk, she began to demonstrate her idea. 'You see, the photograph showed a small wood where the gallery was to be sited. But if the main gallery was put there it would mean felling quite a number of trees, and somehow I wondered if we could avoid that. It's always a shame to cut down trees, isn't it?' She looked up for agreement to the faces round the desk and unfortunately caught Rafe Jordan's eyes, and for some reason found it impossible to look away.

He was smiling a rather unpleasant smile and for once he was meeting her eyes. 'Quite the little conservationist, aren't we, Miss Bennett?' he drawled. 'Do go on.'

She swallowed and dragged her eyes back to her drawing. 'Well, I thought it would be an idea to have the entrance door to the gallery right *in* the wood itself, so that you come on it sort of unexpectedly. It would be made of glass so that it reflected the green of the trees around. Then, inside the door, would be a small lobby or atrium where just one of the principal objects could be placed. Or perhaps one picture. From the lobby a passage would lead between the trees. It would be quite a narrow passage, with display niches along both sides and with either windows or interior lighting, and it would lead into the main gallery, which would be sited in the clearing near the lake. There would be no windows in the gallery—the light would come from the ceiling, which would be entirely of glass—and on a slight rake—like this . . .' she pointed with the pencil. 'At the far end of the gallery this smallish door would open on to a piazza beside the lake, the piazza being as large or as small as the client wished . . .'

Her voice gave out then on a nervous gulp. She had said her say, if they wanted to ridicule it, let them. She waited, curiously calm now.

There was a silence when she finished speaking. She fixed her eyes on a silver-framed photograph on the desk. It was of a very beautiful woman with white hair, holding a small dog in her arms and smiling into the camera.

The senior partner cleared his throat. 'Yes,' he said slowly. 'Yes, I see.' He looked up into Sara's flushed face. 'A very—imaginative piece of work, Sara. Unusual. Somewhat subjective, of course, but none the worse for that.' He turned his head towards his son. 'What do you think, Rafe?'

Rafe Jordan's dark handsome face was expressionless. 'I agree with you, of course, Dad,' he said.

Mr Jordan Senior got to his feet, gathering the four drawings up into one roll. 'Good,' he said in a satisfied way. 'We'll get these packed up and you can take them over to France tomorrow and present them to our good friend Monsieur Savin. At least he'll have a choice—also there's the idea that you put to him yourself when you were there, Rafe. I should think one of the five will appeal to him.' He looked round at the juniors. 'Many thanks, all of you, for the work you've put in. It will all do Jordan's credit,' he added pleasantly.

'What a sweetie he is,' murmured Sara to Bob as they filed back into the design office. 'Not a bit like his son.'

Bob wasn't listening. He looked paler than usual and there was a nervous twitch round his mouth. 'That drawing of yours, Sara . . .'

'Yes?' She grinned at him. 'Did you think it was too—well—fanciful? I'm sure our Rafe did.'

' I thought it was brilliant,' said Bob generously. 'I'll be surprised if it isn't the one that's accepted.'

Sara laughed. 'And I'll be surprised if it is! Bless you, Bob, for those kind words, but I'm not expecting miracles. And if Mr Rafe Jordan is doing the presentation my little effort will be the last one he'll push forward. He's probably thinking up all sorts of snags about the building already.'

Bob shook his head wisely. 'We'll have to wait and see.'

And that, Sara persuaded herself, would be the last she would hear of it. Still, the project had been a joy to work on, and she comforted herself with the senior partner's words. Imaginative, he had said. Daddy would have been pleased about that, she thought, as she lay in bed that night, listening to the rain slashing against the window.

And oh, how she wished he were still here so that she could tell him. Somehow Rafe Jordan's cold disapproval would have been easier to bear if she hadn't been so alone.

CHAPTER TWO

'AH, you're still here, Sara—good.' Donald Jordan walked over to Sara's drawing-table as she got up from her stool, easing her shoulders, pushing away a strand of richly red hair that was straying across her forehead.

'I promise I won't claim overtime,' she smiled. 'I got carried away with the kitchen quarters of the Ferguson house.' She indicated the drawing on her table. 'Woman's work, would you say?' she added teasingly.

That was the nice thing about the senior partner—you could joke with him and he treated you as an equal, or very nearly. Not, she thought dourly, as his son treated her—as something the office cat had brought in.

He bent over the drawing. 'Hm—interesting, I must have a good look at it tomorrow. But there's something even more important I have to tell you this afternoon.' He glanced round the double row of empty drawing-tables. 'Everyone else left? Yes, it seems so. Well, perhaps that's just as well—I'd rather break the news to you in private, Sara.'

Sara went cold all over. This could only mean one thing—the hateful Rafe had been complaining about her to his father, and Donald Jordan, for all his pleasant manner, had evidently decided to end her contract when the month was up.

'N-news?' she stammered, through lips that had suddenly gone dry.

Donald Jordan nodded. 'Good news, I hope you'll agree. Rafe has just been on the phone to me from France. Alain Savin has chosen your plan for the gallery, Sara. He's very enthusiastic about your idea and he's decided to go ahead and work out the possibilities.'

Sara stared stupidly at the big man in front of her. 'Whew!' she breathed at last. 'Do you mind if I sit down?' She sank on to the stool she had just vacated.

Donald Jordan was watching her, small creases fanning out beside his eyes. 'Is it all that much of a surprise?'

She nodded speechlessly, swallowed hard, and then managed to croak, 'Sorry! It'll take a few minutes to sink in.'

He patted her hand in a fatherly fashion. 'Come and sit down in my office and get your breath back.'

He pushed open the door, indicating the large leather chair reserved for clients. Then he went over to a cupboard and came back to her with a glass in each hand. 'Sherry,' he smiled. 'We should drink to this, surely?'

He carried his own glass to his chair behind the desk. 'I'm very pleased, Sara, for the firm as well as for you. It's quite a new venture for us—up to now our work has been mostly domestic, as you know. But if we get a reputation for imaginative work in an arts context it may well open up a whole new area.' He lifted his glass towards her. 'Be that as it may, here's to the Alain Savin Gallery.'

Sara took a gulp of the sherry and felt better. She had just realised that a marvellous surprise could upset you as much as a devastating one.

'I'm sorry to be so stupid,' she said shakily. 'It was just—I never really believed I had a chance. I saw Bob's drawing and it was so—so professional. Beside it, mine seemed amateurish.'

Donald Jordan nodded. 'Bob Stratton's work *is* highly professional and meticulous. No doubt we shall call on his skills at a later stage in the project. But at this stage it's the idea that counts—and the idea is yours, Sara.'

'Not even your son's?' Sara ventured.

He shook his head, smiling at her in an odd way. 'Not even Rafe's,' he said. 'He tackled it from quite a different direction. He'll probably tell you when you get over there.'

Sara frowned. 'When I get over there? I don't understand . . .'

'No, of course not, I should have explained. Alain Savin wants you there as soon as possible, Sara, to go into your ideas in more detail. He'll set up an office for you in the hotel and you can do a series of schematic design sketches for him. Have you ever done any three-dimensional models?'

'Yes, I worked on a few for Mr Field. It was fascinating.'

'Good, well, that's another option.' He looked seriously at her across the desk. 'This is your big chance, Sara, and I'm sure you'll make the most of it. Now, as for plans,' he went on briskly, 'I'll have a flight to Paris booked for you for Friday. Your passport's in order? Yes? It'll be a relief when we don't have to bother with them, won't it? I'll arrange with Rafe to meet you at Charles de Gaulle Airport. The Savin hotel is rather in the middle of nowhere, I gather, but Rafe took his own car over with him, so there's no problem there. Take a few pretty dresses with you—the hotel is fairly luxurious, from what Rafe says.'

Sara frowned faintly. 'Will—will your son be staying on there?'

Donald Jordan studied her face thoughtfully before he replied. Then he said, a little wryly, 'For a time—yes. I'm afraid you'll have to put up with him, Sara. He's not in the best of moods just now—for personal reasons. But I think you'll find him co-operative and helpful to work with in any matter that concerns the firm.'

'Yes, of course,' Sara said quickly. Her eyes met those of the senior partner and she had the feeling that he understood what was going through her mind. 'I'm sure we'll get along very well.'

'*I'm* sure you will.' Donald Jordan stood up. 'Take tomorrow off to get packed up and so on. I'll have details of your flight and tickets sent to your address tomorrow afternoon. Right?'

'Right,' Sara said rather faintly, and took the hand he held out.

'Good luck, Sara,' said the senior partner. 'I'll look forward to hearing all about it when you return.'

As Sara waited among the crowd round the conveyor belt for her luggage to appear at Charles de Gaulle airport on Friday afternoon, she felt tears prick behind her eyes. It was all so familiar, and she almost expected to see Daddy waiting for her when she got through Customs, his soft-brimmed hat pulled down over his eyes, his hands stuck into the pockets of his baggy jacket.

The years when his studio was in Paris, before they moved back to England, had been good years in lots of ways. Sara had been studying in London, but every vacation had been spent here in the rambling studio apartment, and she had grown to love France like a second home. Her father's artist friends were delighted to have a pretty young girl added to their circle, and she enjoyed the concerts, the informal parties, the picnics in the woods outside the city. Most of all she enjoyed wandering round the shady, flower-filled gardens or lingering in the pavement cafés, drinking coffee and talking—mostly about art.

For a short time she had played with the idea of being an artist herself, until it became clear that she would never be anything but third-rate, and that didn't suit Sara at all. But in her father's studio she had learned a lot about draughtsmanship, so when she finally decided on architecture as her chosen career she had a head start, finally qualifying with a very good degree.

The heady feeling that came with success kindled in her as she thought now that she was really on her way in that career. She could still hardly believe that her drawing had been chosen by this Monsieur Savin for his gallery. It was amazing and wonderful, and she was going to do the very best she could to build on this beginning. Rafe Jordan would no doubt be none too pleased to see her arrive, but she would keep her cool and remind herself that this was a professional assignment and she could afford to ignore his disagreeable attitude towards her.

Ah! Here was her luggage coming round at last. As she leaned forward to grab the bulky travelling bag and heave it on to her trolley she heard a sudden squeal from somewhere on her right. A harassed-looking woman walking beside her was in all sorts of difficulties. The three bulging suitcases she had balanced precariously on her trolley were slipping sideways, and a small girl in a pink dress sitting on top of them was in danger of being deposited between the feet of the hurrying crowd of passengers. The woman made an ineffective grab at the child as the worst happened. The cases overbalanced and the little girl with them. She yelled in fright as she tipped over, her little arms waving in the air.

Sara let go of her own trolley and managed to grab the child just as she lost her balance. A couple of passers-by stopped to help. The bags were replaced on the trolley while the woman flapped rather helplessly, and the little girl clung round Sara's neck with surprising strength for one so small.

The woman smiled wanly. '*Merci, mademoiselle.*' She reached for the little girl to plant her back on top of the luggage, but the child had had quite enough of that mode of transport. She hung on to Sara like a small monkey.

'I'll take her if you like, I can push my trolley with one hand,' Sara offered, glad of the years she had spent in France that had given her a good command of the language. 'It's not far to Customs—we'll keep together. Are you being met?'

The woman was flustered in her gratitude. 'I hope so . . . my husband . . . it is so good of you . . .'

Together they passed through Customs, the woman moaning on about the horrors of her journey all the way from Scotland. After that they were confronted by seas of faces eagerly scanning incoming passengers. Sara's companion had spotted her husband and pushed forward into the crush, calling out to him. The little girl, seeing her mother disappear, put up a wild yell, and Sara hung on tight to her, let go of her trolley and followed at a run.

At last everything was sorted out with compliments on both sides, and Sara couldn't resist giving the thin little body a final hug before she handed the child over. She stood looking after the family as they made their way across the arrivals lounge. The woman was smiling and laughing now—quite a different person—talking twenty-nine to the dozen, while her husband pushed the loaded trolley with one hand, the other holding the little girl perched on his shoulder. Sara sighed. It was nice to see a really happy family, delighting in each other.

Then she remembered her trolley and whirled round, almost colliding with a tall figure that barred her way. 'What was all that about?' said Rafe Jordan, frowning not at all welcomingly.

Sara blinked at him. And then an unexpected thing happened. At the sudden sight of him standing quite still, tall and somehow formidable in the midst of the milling crowd of people, she was aware of an odd gripping sensation behind her ribs, a sensation that was almost pain. It passed in a moment and she met his unsmiling gaze with a faint lift of her brows.

'A woman having trouble with her luggage. I was able to help.' Her mouth soft, she glanced after the family, fast disappearing among the crowd. 'The little girl was so sweet—like a Dutch doll, with her fringe and her great big eyes.'

He ignored that completely. 'Let's get going,' he said impatiently. 'I've been hanging about waiting here for the best part of an hour.'

'Sorry,' Sara said distantly. Nothing had changed; he was still as unfriendly as ever. 'The flight was late on take-off, and then there was a hold-up at baggage collection.'

He looked darkly at the large travelling case on her trolley. 'Couldn't you have managed with hand luggage?'

'No, I couldn't,' said Sara, equally frosty. 'Your father told me I'd need to come prepared for a stay at the hotel.'

He heaved the heavy bag off the trolley. 'I hope he also explained that you've come here to work. Come along, I've got my car in a short-stay park.'

He set off at a furious pace and she almost had to run to keep up with him. Along passages, into lifts, then more passages, round corners. He carried her bag as if it weighed ounces rather than pounds, until finally he reached a sleek black Mercedes, a gleaming aristocrat among the ranks of parked cars, and unlocked the door. He tossed the bag on the back seat and got in behind the wheel, making no attempt to open the passenger door for Sara.

Surly brute, she thought, breathing rather fast from the rush through the air terminal. Just because he'd had to wait for a few minutes! He really was the most arrogant, unpleasant man she'd ever come across. She climbed into the car and fastened her seat-belt. I won't speak to him again, she vowed. I'll keep absolutely silent until he speaks first—if he ever does.

She sat stiffly on the soft leather seat, hugging her in-flight bag on her knee. She had hoped that Rafe Jordan would be, if not friendly, then less aggressive towards her than he had been in London, but it looked as if that hope was vain. How on earth was she going to work with him if he kept up this attitude?

From the way he drove the Mercedes, with hair-raising impatience, he might have been a born Parisian. Sara realised with a faint sinking feeling that he was making for the *périphérique*, the circular roadway round Paris—that formidable test of driving which even seasoned drivers often avoided if they could. She needn't have worried. Glancing up at the narrowed eyes and the firm set of his mouth, she saw that he was enjoying the challenge of weaving crazily in and out of the traffic. She had to admit that he drove with the utmost flair and confidence, but all the same she breathed a sigh of relief when they were finally off the circular road and speeding down a motorway.

'Where are we making for?' Sara broke her vow of silence. She had no intention of chatting, but it would be nice to know how long they were likely to be on the way. She was fighting back a faintly disturbed feeling inside, which might be a delayed travel sickness. Or it might be the result of sitting so close to this large, formidable man in the intimacy of the car.

'The Loire valley,' he said shortly.

'But that'll take hours and hours!' Sara couldn't hide her dismay.

He flicked her a glance. 'I'll do my best to entertain *mademoiselle* on the journey.' He touched a button on the dashboard and the strains of Mozart flooded out sweetly from the quadruple speakers.

'Sorry I haven't anything more—er—youthful to offer you,' he said, not sounding in the least sorry.

'What do you mean—youthful?'

'Well, I suppose rock—or pop—would appeal more to one of your tender years,' he drawled.

He had brought sarcasm to a fine art, hadn't he? Was there no limit to the man's studied offensiveness?

'I'd call this music fairly youthful,' she said, hanging on to her temper with an effort. 'I shouldn't be surprised if all the kids whistled the tune in the street in Mozart's time. And he was only a kid himself when he composed it,' she added. 'Fifteen, wasn't he?'

From the corner of her eye she saw his head turn briefly towards her. 'You're very knowledgeable, Miss Bennett,' he said drily.

Suddenly Sara had had enough. An effort must be made if she was going to get through the next few days without being goaded into making a physical attack on this insufferable man. 'And you're very stiff-necked, Mr Jordan,' she replied with equal dryness. 'Couldn't you manage to relax sufficiently to call me Sara? Everyone else in the office does, including your father.'

There was a long silence. At last he said, 'Would it mean anything to you if I told you I find it totally impossible to relax in your presence?'

Sara gave her head a little shake. Had she heard him aright? Yes, she had—there was no way she could have been mistaken. She frowned slightly. 'No, I'm afraid it doesn't mean a thing to me. I don't understand what it is about me that has such an unfortunate effect on you. But as we're apparently going to have to work together for a time, you'd better spell it out, and if I have any habits that irritate you I'll see what I can do about them. For the sake of the firm, of course.' *That* should bring him out into the open, she thought with a certain satisfaction.

He made no reply at all to that. She stole a glance at the handsome profile. Carved in stone, she thought. He might have been a Roman statue for all the response she was getting to her challenge.

Oh, well, I'll have to try again later on, she thought, concentrating on the music and fixing her gaze determinedly through the side window as the car pursued its way through the outskirts of Paris and finally out into countryside. They must have been driving for nearly an hour when Rafe finally turned off the motorway at an exit.

'Are we nearly there?' queried Sara in surprise. She'd imagined it would be much further off the beaten track than this.

'No,' said Rafe. 'We're not.'

The country road was a blessed relief after the busy motorway. Quiet and empty of traffic. There were few trees, and the fields—French fields always seemed so enormous after neat English ones—stretched away into the far distance. Rafe drew the car on to a verge and shut off the engine.

'We'd better get this straightened out now,' he said. He sounded tense and almost angry. 'To reply to your last question, yes, you do have an unfortunate effect on me. You have done from the moment I saw you in the design office. You're too bloody tempting for my peace of mind.'

Sara gasped. Whatever she had been expecting it wasn't this. 'I don't understand—I've done nothing whatever to deserve a remark like that. Tempting!' She flung the word at him indignantly. 'What are you accusing me of—trying to seduce you? I wouldn't try to seduce any man, and even if I did you'd be the very last . . .'

He turned his head, and as she met his eyes she saw something there that took her breath away completely. 'You don't have to try, Sara.' His voice was husky, sending a shock-wave rippling through her whole body. Her eyes widened as his arm went round her and his mouth came down to hers in a long, hard, hungry kiss.

She was too amazed to resist, and anyway, the arm that held her was iron-hard against her warm softness. Also, after the first shock she found she was enjoying his kiss. His lips were firm against hers, and she liked that; he wasn't greedily probing her mouth, it seemed as if he simply wanted the feel of it against his. Sara felt her own mouth relax, and then, and then only, did his tongue take advantage of her parted lips and thrust forward, with a rhythmical surge that patterned a more intimate movement. She felt a deep throb of arousal and for a crazy moment wanted to link her arms round his neck and draw him closer, wanted to press herself against him.

Then sanity prevailed. 'No!' She pushed him away with all her might and he sank back into the driving seat as if the strength had gone out of him. They sat in silence except for the sound of their quickened breathing.

Rafe was the first to speak. 'See?' he said bitterly. 'That's the effect you have on me.'

'What am I supposed to do?' Sara's voice was shaky. 'Apologise?'

'Don't be silly,' he said impatiently. 'It's not your fault.'

She sighed. 'I really don't understand. Couldn't you explain a little? I know I'm not a *femme fatale*, or even a Marilyn Monroe, to have every man in sight lusting for me.'

'You're very attractive,' he said in a helpless kind of way. 'You must have plenty of boyfriends. Isn't there one special one?'

'Not at the moment. Which doesn't mean I'm available.'

'No, of course not.' He made an impatient movement. 'God, this is a ridiculous conversation!'

'Just what I was thinking myself.' Sara folded her hands in her lap and gazed out across the fields. She was pleased that her voice was so steady, because in truth she was still churning inside as a result of that moment of madness.

'Look, Sara,' Rafe said at last, as if he were hanging on to his patience by an effort, 'do you mind if we leave it there for the moment without going into any convoluted explanations? If I alarmed you or annoyed you I apologise. You needn't be afraid that I'll pounce on you at the first opportunity. It was just—one of those things. Can you pretend it didn't happen?'

'I suppose so,' Sara mumbled. She didn't want to pretend it hadn't happened. It was deeply humiliating to have to admit it to herself, but what she wanted was for him to put his arms round her and kiss her again. 'Can we get on now, please?'

He didn't say anything more, just stared straight ahead and drove with a kind of quiet desperation until they joined the motorway again, and then covered mile after mile with such violent speed that Sara clutched the edge of her seat, too scared even to think about what had happened, until finally the big car nosed its way briefly and more sedately along narrow roads and turned into a twisting drive flanked by high shrubs, to pull up eventually in a wide forecourt in front of a great grey stone building.

By this time dusk was falling and lights glittered from the windows. Two castellated towers stood out darkly against the pale evening sky. The wide arch of the entrance could once have housed a drawbridge across which knights in armour rode their white chargers. The hotel looked like a fairy-tale castle, Sara thought. A place where miraculous things happened. Ogres and handsome princes and imprisoned maidens wouldn't come amiss here. No prizes for guessing who the chief ogre might be, she thought with a grin.

A uniformed porter ran swiftly down the steps and took their travelling bags, and they followed him into a high-ceilinged, spacious lounge with a reception desk at the far end. Looking around her, Sara thought that Mr Jordan Senior had been right. This was a very upmarket establishment indeed. One or two of the low tables were occupied by elegantly dressed people. Flowers were everywhere, their scent hanging on the air. Great crystal chandeliers drooped from the lofty ceiling. The place was more like the inside of a cathedral than a hotel, she thought. Except, of course, that no cathedral had this ankle-thick carpeting and deep lounge seats and atmosphere of plush luxury.

A tall, thin man came swiftly towards them, both hands outstretched, smiling a welcome. He wore an impeccably cut grey suit, his hair was cut short and slightly grizzled, and he might have been any age between forty and sixty. 'Rafe, my friend, you have returned with your colleague. That is very good.' He spoke in French and saluted Sara by kissing her on both cheeks as Rafe made the introduction, holding both her hands a little longer, perhaps, than was necessary at a first meeting and smiling at her with warm brown eyes. But Alain Savin was so immediately friendly, so obviously delighted to meet her that she found herself smiling back her widest, prettiest smile.

'*Enchanté, mademoiselle.*' Alain turned to Rafe, his eyes gleaming wickedly. 'I did not know, Rafe, that you had such delightful young ladies working at your establishment. It is so lucky that she should be the one who has designed such a superb gallery for me.' He continued to speak in French.

Sara looked at Rafe. Would politeness force him to agree reluctantly with this somewhat fulsome praise?

She might have known! Politeness wasn't Rafe Jordan's strong suit. 'Sara is well qualified, Alain, and I'm sure she will be capable of meeting your requirements,' he said stiffly.

Sara smiled to herself. True to form, she thought. What was that saying—'damning with faint praise'? This must be it.

Alain turned back to Sara. 'There is—much—to talk of.' He smiled apologetically. 'My English is not vairy good.'

'Don't worry,' said Sara, speaking in French with her best Parisian accent. 'We shall speak in your language.' She heard Rafe's quick intake of breath beside her. Did I surprise you, Mr Rafe Jordan? she thought, aware of a small feeling of satisfaction. That evens things up a bit, then—goodness knows, you surprised me a little while ago!

Alain Savin was obviously delighted that he would not have to struggle with his English. In fact, he seemed delighted with Sara in every possible way, and showed it with true Gallic courtesy. Compliments flowed from his lips as he led them across to the reception desk. Rafe, thought Sara, stealing a glance at his dark frowning face as he signed the book, was definitely not amused. Perhaps he would go back to London, and leave her to work with this pleasant Frenchman, who had such beautiful manners. Not a hope, of course; he wouldn't trust her with the working-up of her drawings for the gallery, however much he resented her presence.

'You will both join me for a drink before you go to your rooms?' Alain Savin led them to one of the low tables with crimson velvet lounge chairs. 'I insist. After all that travel...' He turned to Sara and helped her off with her loose jacket, enquiring about her journey, and she chatted away happily to him as a waiter arrived with their drinks. She was enjoying speaking French again, and Alain was obviously enjoying listening to her, sitting beside her, smiling, leaning towards her, brown eyes dancing. Rafe lay back in his chair watching them, an expression that could only be called sardonic on his handsome face.

A beep-beep sounded from Alain's breast pocket and brought him to his feet. 'Duty calls.' He pulled an apologetic face. 'I am wanted in the office. I will send Gaston to show you to your rooms. I have moved you to the annexe, Rafe, so that you can both have rooms there. You will, I think, wish to be near together——' he smiled blandly from one to the other of them '——for the convenience of working, of course. I will see you at dinner, *oui*?' He hurried away across the lounge and a moment later the porter who had brought in their luggage appeared beside the table. 'If you will please follow me,' he said politely, and Rafe murmured to Sara, with a touch of irony, 'You are now about to witness a completed Jordan masterpiece. Our firm designed the annexe a few years ago.' He slung Sara's jacket over his arm and put a hand at her elbow as they followed the porter across the lounge, through a door and into a square hall with doors on either side. The touch of his hand on her bare skin made her nerve-ends tingle. She couldn't very well pull away, because he was merely being courteous, but she wished he wouldn't touch her.

The porter indicated a large bedroom—evidently a double room—richly furnished, with a four-poster bed hung with drapery in a deep turquoise blue, the same colour as the velvet curtains which covered the long windows. Heavy mahogany wardrobe cupboards lined one side of the room. There was a writing-desk of the same dark wood, a chaise-longue and two elegant, tapestry-upholstered chairs. Prints and maps and gold-framed mirrors and embroidered hangings adorned the walls. Sara's travelling bag had been put on a stand at the foot of the bed.

She stood looking round, bemused. 'Is this really my room?' she said when the porter had retired. 'I should prefer something less—spectacular. I shall feel like Marie Antoinette if I have to sleep here!' She heard herself giggle rather nervously.

Rafe was standing watching her. He had an unnerving habit of just watching her in complete silence. 'Expecting to be led to the guillotine tomorrow morning?'

'Something like that,' she mumbled. Well, at least he had made a joke, of sorts. It lightened the atmosphere.

'I think Alain would be mortally offended if you asked for another room,' he said. 'Obviously he would consider this entirely suitable for his *protégée*—for that is obviously what you have become already. In common parlance, you've made a hit there, Sara.'

She glared at him. 'It's a very pleasant change to be treated as if I'm a human being and not some sort of—of lower form of life!'

Rafe stuck both hands in his pockets, still regarding her fixedly, his lips twisting a fraction. 'Referring to my—er—less than cordial welcome of you to the firm?'

'Yes, of course I am.' Suddenly all Sara's pent-up indignation of the last fortnight welled up as she confronted the formidable man standing so still in front of her. 'You've been a perfect beast to me since you walked into the office that first day; you've never missed an opportunity of showing me how much you dislike me. I couldn't help hearing what you said to your father. "Did you have to take on a girl like that, Dad?" you said. *Why*?' she blurted out, thoroughly worked up by now. 'What is it about me, for goodness' sake? A girl like *what*?'

Rafe moved forward until he was standing close in front of her. Then to her utter confusion he reached out and took a strand of her richly red hair between finger and thumb. 'A girl with hair the colour of yours,' he said in an odd, strained voice.

'You're allergic to carrots?' she said with awful flippancy.

'*Carrots*? Don't be stupid, carrots don't come in this colour. This gorgeous—dark——' He was twisting the strand round his finger, staring at it, his face bleak. 'Pomegranate seeds, perhaps. And I've seen a wine this colour—a highly intoxicating brew.'

Sara swallowed hard to stop herself blurting out some facetious retort. There was something here that she didn't understand, and it had nothing to do with her. That was the first thing that entered her mind. The second was that he was standing much too close and she sensed the tension in him, just the same sort of tension that had led to that devastating kiss in the car. She felt a shiver run through her.

Play it light, she thought. She moved back and his hand dropped to his side. 'Well, if my hair's my only crime I could change the colour while we're here—it might help you to tolerate my presence. I'm sure the hotel has a first-class hairdresser. Blonde, black, silver—what's your fancy?'

It was an unfortunate choice of words. Rafe's dark brows drew together ominously and he advanced closer, making her back away until she came up against the wardrobe and couldn't back any further. Both his hands were on her shoulders and he shook her not very gently. 'At the moment, Sara, my fancy is you. So be careful, I'm not in the easiest of moods just now.'

He was much too close. She could see the pulse that moved at his temple, smell the clean male smell of him, feel his breath on her cheek. A tremor of something that felt like fear contracted the lower part of her inside. but it might not have been fear—it might have been something quite embarrassingly different. Whatever it was, she needed to detach herself from his grip as quickly as possible. She slid sideways out of his grasp and sank into a chair, her knees like rubber under her.

Thoughts were skittering round in Sara's head. Somewhere in Rafe's recent past was a woman with red hair—a woman who had aroused either his love or his hate, or probably both. She must certainly have aroused his passion and he was tempted to take it out on her—Sara.

'OK,' she said rather shakily, 'I think I get the message. But I wasn't being completely frivolous when I suggested changing the colour of my hair while we're here. I still think it might be a good idea. I'll have to consider it.'

He loomed over her. 'Don't you dare,' he growled. 'You certainly won't dye your hair on my account.'

'My hair is my own,' she told him crisply, her usual spirit returning. 'I shall do exactly what I like—or think best—about it. And, by the way, you don't call it dyeing these days, you know. The word has crude overtones of peroxide and henna. Colouring—tinting—sounds more subtle, wouldn't you say?'

She got carefully to her feet and found with relief that her legs would support her. 'Now may we change the subject, please? If I'm to have this palatial room as my bedroom I'd like to know where I am to work.'

She didn't look at him as she spoke. She knew she had riled him and she guessed that he was torn between behaving in the civilised manner that their professional relationship demanded, and throwing her on the bed and taking out on her the savage rage that seethed just below the surface.

She heard him draw in a deep breath and then he walked quickly across the room and threw open a door on the opposite side of the hall. 'I'll have a work-table put in here for you,' he said. 'I'll see you have everything you'll need.'

He led the way into an even larger room—evidently a living-room. It was a beautiful room, comfortable without being in the least fussy. A room furnished by two people in close sympathy with each other, as Alain and his wife must have been. The shaggy ivory carpet matched the squashy leather chairs and sofas. For the rest, the room was furnished with lovingly chosen collector's items: low marquetry tables, an elaborate Chinese cupboard, an antique secretaire, its brass handles shining against dark wood polished to satiny smoothness. A small table with carved legs, and two mahogany dining chairs stood before the long window, and in the darkest corner of the room an elaborate flower arrangement in a pottery jug glowed like a medley of jewels.

'As you may gather,' said Rafe, 'these rooms form part of a suite. That's the way we designed it, to Alain's instructions, when we built the annexe. The intention was that he and his wife should have the annexe as their private living quarters when he made the château into a hotel. He was devoted to his wife, poor fellow—nothing was too good for her,' he added rather woodenly.

Oh dear, thought Sara, we've touched on another sore spot. I wish I knew something about this man's ex-wife—whether he loved her or hated her. Whether he was torn apart by the divorce or welcomed it as a relief from impossible strain.

She said quickly, to change the subject of the conversation from wives to something safer, 'It's a beautiful suite. I love the loftiness of the rooms and the sense of space. You must have had a lot of satisfaction from the contract—did you do the design yourself?'

'All my own work.' The touch of irony in his voice warned her against being too fulsome in her appreciation.

'Was it difficult? It must have been quite a challenge to add on an extension to a building as old as this one.'

'It was hellishly difficult, believe me.' He rubbed his neck as if he were recalling the snags that had arisen. Then he started prowling round the big room, examining the pictures hanging on the walls, the *objets d'art* arranged in a glass-fronted display cabinet. 'The thing was that the château was built on the site of a medieval fortified castle—some of the original building still remains, as you'll see when you get outside in the daylight tomorrow. The castle originally had a moat round it, you see. The drainage problems were horrendous and——'

'Oh!' squeaked Sara. 'I must have second sight. When we drove up I couldn't help imagining the entrance door with a drawbridge over a moat. I thought I was merely being romantic.'

He stopped prowling and gave her a cool look. 'But then you *are* a romantic, aren't you, Miss Sara Bennett? Your design for Alain's gallery confirms that.'

She frowned. 'Am I? I didn't think I was. I thought I was a modern, both-feet-on-the-ground girl. That's how I see myself.'

'We don't see ourselves as others see us—which is perhaps just as well,' Rafe said grimly.

'About the gallery——' Sara sank into one of the deep lounge chairs and made a bid to steer the conversation away from personal matters, to which it seemed to have a nasty habit of returning. If she could get him sitting down and talking about the profession they shared it might tend to ease the situation. 'I was wondering about the practical side—are there local consultants we can use or shall we have to rely on some of the big firms in Paris?'

Rafe continued to prowl. 'Oh, it's early days to be thinking along those lines. Let's get the preliminaries over first—we've still got to choose and survey a site.' He was examining an oil painting— a landscape with figures, a girl on a horse, a man walking beside her. 'Alain has several works by Salvator Rosa. They'll make a nice romantic group for your gallery.' His mouth twisted, more contemptuously than teasingly.

Sara gave it up. 'It isn't only women who can be bitchy,' she said shortly, getting to her feet again. She turned towards the door into the bedroom. 'I'd like a shower before dinner. Is there a bathroom en suite?'

'Sort of,' said Rafe. 'I'll show you.' He led the way back into the bedroom, and crossed it to a door which opened into a bathroom. Sara caught a glimpse of an enormous ivory-coloured bath lavishly painted in a flower pattern picked out in gold. Just as you'd expect, she thought. No expense spared.

'I'm afraid we'll have to share the bathroom,' Rafe said matter-of-factly. 'It's a nuisance, but there it is. We'll come to some sort of civilised arrangement, I'm sure. This is the way Alain wanted the rooms arranged. He and his wife were very—close, as I expect you've already gathered. You can have the shower first,' he added, 'I'll be getting unpacked.'

'Where's your room?' Sara asked. She and Rafe Jordan were certainly *not* very close, and it was maddening to have to share a suite designed for a loving, intimate married couple. She remembered the way Alain had said, 'You will, I think, wish to be near together,' and felt the blood surge into her face. Was there only one bedroom? She glanced at the huge four-poster bed and looked away again quickly. Surely he couldn't have meant . . . surely he didn't think . . .

'Don't worry, Sara,' Rafe drawled, his eyes on her hot cheeks. 'There's a dressing-room communicating on the other side of the bathroom. I shall occupy my chaste couch in there. It seems that there are no locks on the doors. You'll just have to trust me. Let me know when you've finished with the shower.' He opened a door on the opposite side of the bathroom and disappeared into the room beyond.

Sara began to unpack her travelling bags, thrusting back her resentment, reminding herself that she was a professional and that there were bound to be snags about any job. But the snag about this one, she thought grimly as she hung up her pretty dresses in the closet, wasn't anything as simple as an ancient moat to be drained.

The snag was a maddening, mystifying—*man*. A man who was determined to take out on her some grudge against her sex—especially a member of her sex who happened to have red hair. She stared at herself in the triple mirror on the dressing-table, touching the silky strand he had touched. The colour of pomegranate seeds, he had said.

Who's the romantic now, Mr Rafe Jordan? she asked her reflection, and pulled a face at herself.

But of course he wasn't really referring to *her* hair—he was remembering some other female. Think of that, Sara, and don't get too interested in the man, or let yourself get too angry with him. Remember this is a professional assignment and keep him at arm's length.

She just wished she could forget how it felt when he had kissed her in the car. And she had to try to ignore a curious weakness that invaded her limbs as she undressed and stepped inside the glass-fronted shower cubicle.

CHAPTER THREE

SARA stood under the shower and let the cool water flow soothingly over her hot body as she contemplated the embarrassing situation she found herself in. She wondered if she could ask Alain Savin for a different room, but no, that wasn't practicable, there were too many unknown factors.

Did Monsieur Savin really believe that she and Rafe were sleeping together? She supposed it might be quite a common situation—a man and a girl working as a team abroad, both unattached, or at least unmarried! But it wasn't the sort of situation she would consider for a moment. Especially with a man she disliked and resented, a man who never lost an opportunity to treat her with sarcastic, hurtful . . . nastiness. He really was a hateful man. And yet . . . and yet . . .

That kiss! He had kissed her from simple male need, that was all. But whatever the reason, one part of her had to admit that it had certainly made the earth shake a little for her. She had never been kissed quite like that before, she thought, soaping herself luxuriously all over with the most heavenly scented soap. You'd think, wouldn't you, that a kiss is a kiss is a kiss? But not so. In Sara's fairly limited experience no two men's kisses were alike at all.

Thoughtfully she rinsed off the creamy lather, caressing her smooth limbs as the water pricked in tiny jets against her skin. One thing she was sure of—she would recognise Rafe Jordan's kiss if it ever happened again . . .

A short rap on the door of the dressing-room made her jump. 'How much longer are you going to be in there?' came Rafe's voice, irritable as usual.

Sara resisted the sorry-I-won't-be-much-longer reply she would have given to any reasonable person. She had to fight her corner all the time against this man or he would grind her into the ground. 'About another five minutes or so,' she called back coolly, and heard a grunt from the other side of the door.

She stepped out of the shower and dried herself slowly and thoroughly on one of the soft almond-green bath towels. There was a complete selection of toiletries on a tinted glass shelf, and she helped herself liberally to toilet water. Um . . . lovely! *Very* French! A dusting of powder with the same exclusive label and she was ready to slip into her flimsy nylon robe and tie the belt tightly before she tapped on the communicating door, singing out, 'All clear now.'

'About time too!' Rafe came charging in almost before she was out of the bathroom, and the words that followed reached her clearly as he muttered under his breath, 'Phew! The place smells like a brothel.'

Sara paused for a second. 'Of course, *you'd* know all about that, wouldn't you?' she said sweetly, and closed the door with a firm click.

Back in her own room she found she was breathing rather fast. But at least she had kept her end up, and in a way it had been rather pleasurable. It seemed to mark a certain change in their relationship. They had sparred like a couple who knew each other very well—almost like husband and wife. She grinned to herself. There it was—the word 'wife' again! She must forget about wives, ex or otherwise, in her dealings with Rafe Jordan.

Now for something to wear for dinner. She slid back the door of the huge wardrobe-cupboard and surveyed her modest number of garments—three dresses, three pair of jeans, assorted tops, the white linen suit she had travelled in, a couple of blouses and a long amber velvet skirt that was a favourite of hers. Together they didn't fill a tenth of the space. Alain Savin's wife must have been the possessor of a fabulous selection of clothes. She was probably very sophisticated—like Alain himself. Everything Sara had heard and seen of him—which wasn't very much!—suggested to her that he was a most interesting man. She was looking forward to talking to him.

She wished she knew if the guests here dressed up for dinner. Probably they did. Oh, well, she wasn't going to compete. She was a business girl, here on business, not one of the well-heeled customers of this luxury hotel.

She selected the simplest of her dresses—a crisp ice-blue cotton, sleeveless, with a cross-over bodice and a skirt that hugged her hips and fluted discreetly just below the knees. She put on light make-up, mostly on eyes and lips, and brushed her hair until it shone like—like pomegranate seeds, she thought, with a wry grin at her reflection. With a last glance into the wood-framed cheval mirror she crossed the hall into the living-room and sat very straight on one of the carved high-backed chairs beside the table. At least the abominable Rafe wouldn't be able to accuse her of keeping him waiting again!

She only just made it—he appeared within minutes,

and at the sight of him, in close-fitting dark trousers and a silky white shirt, open at the neck, she felt again that odd, gripping sensation behind her ribs that she had felt when she saw him at the airport.

'Ready to eat?' he said brusquely.

'Starving,' she admitted.

'Right. Let's go, then.'

As they made their way to the dining-room, through the lounge and along a wide passage, Sara said, 'I wasn't sure what to wear—is it formal dress for dinner?'

Rafe flicked a glance at her and away again quickly. 'You're OK,' he said.

She giggled. He really was too predictable for words! 'Thank you *very* much.' Two could play the sarcasm game.

He stopped abruptly beside a niche holding a fat, decorated ceramic jug—another of the items for the gallery, Sara supposed. At first she thought he was going to talk about it, but instead he was looking at her with a strange expression, dark eyes travelling downwards, from her head to her feet. Sara felt the heat suffusing her whole body and her breath stuck in her throat. His dark, moody eyes seemed to make her aware of herself as he must see her. They seemed to touch her smooth hair gently, linger over the discreet cleavage of her bodice and stroke with slow sensuousness the length of her silky legs to her feet in their strappy white kid sandals.

'What would you like me to say?' His voice was angry. 'Would you prefer me to say that I think you look altogether delectable and desirable and I'd very much like to pick you up and carry you back to my bed at this moment? Satisfied?'

Sara fixed her gaze on the pottery jug which seemed to revolve before her eyes and then right itself. 'At least it would be more—human,' she managed to retort. 'But of course I wouldn't expect you to—to perjure yourself.'

'I don't intend to,' he snapped, and walked on rapidly into the dining-room.

Sara pattered after him. This was a *very* good start to a meal, she thought, as a waiter in a white jacket greeted them and showed them to a side table for two behind a potted plant with curly, glossy leaves. Rafe Jordan managed to churn her up inside and she wondered if she would be able to eat anything at all. But when the huge menu card was handed to her she found her appetite returning. She was darned if she was going to let the man spoil her dinner.

They agreed on *crudités* for starters, then Rafe briskly chose a steak while Sara took her time making her choice. Eventually she settled on duck *à l'orange*. She didn't know whether she would be paying her way for food while she was here. She would have to take that up later.

The ordering of the wine she left to Rafe, of course—she wasn't particularly keen on wine, although she had picked up a fair knowledge of the subject when she lived in Paris. When the wine waiter reverently poured a little into Rafe's glass for the usual ritual of tasting and approving she saw with faint shock that he had ordered a red wine which was, indeed, very close to the colour of her hair.

Rafe nodded to the waiter and both their glasses were filled. When he had gone Rafe picked up his glass and gazed into its depths. 'You didn't believe me, did you?'

he said mockingly.

She didn't pretend that she didn't know what he was talking about. 'To tell the truth, I didn't give the matter any particular thought,' she said without interest, looking round at the other tables, which were filling up now with elegantly dressed women and their escorts. 'Your father told me this was a very upmarket establishment, and he was certainly right. All the "beautiful people" seem to be here.'

Rafe glanced briefly at the occupants of the other tables. 'The décor's more interesting than the diners,' he said, unfolding his napkin. 'There's a lot of the original Renaissance stucco-work in this room. Alain had it restored last year; it was in pretty bad shape when he bought the château. Look at that ceiling, for instance.' He gestured upwards where a cornucopia of flowers and fruits spilled down from the ornamental cornice into the frieze at each corner of the room.

Sara obediently surveyed the elaborate decoration and nodded. 'Beautiful!'

She applied herself to her *crudités* with a faint feeling of relief. At least Rafe had deigned to talk to her about something that interested him.

She said, 'Did you say Monsieur Savin *bought* the château? I somehow had an idea that it came down to him from his ancestors. He seems sort of—well, aristocratic—cultured, if that word hasn't been too overdone.'

Rafe eyed her with faint cynicism. 'A mutual admiration society, I see. Got him in your sights, have you? Oh, no, Alain's not one of the landed gentry, he's a very clever businessman. Extremely well heeled, you'll be interested to know—owns several successful hotels around the country. As for culture—he's something of an authority on Japanese *netsukes*, he has an imposing collection. The little carved button-like ornaments worn by——'

'Yes, I know what *netsukes* are,' Sara interrupted crisply, white teeth biting into a sliver of carrot. *Got him in your sights*? What a nasty gibe—totally unfounded, too! Rafe's sociable approach hadn't lasted long, had it?

'I'd love to see Monsieur Savin's collection,' she said, and added innocently, 'What a nice man he is—I thought him perfectly charming.' That was quite true. She liked what she had seen of Alain Savin very much and she was sure that she was going to get along splendidly with him. Best of all, she had an idea that he might be a very useful ally if she found Rafe's nasty temper too difficult to put up with.

As the waiter arrived with Rafe's *tournedos Chasseur* and her duck *à l'orange* she saw the black frown that had settled between Rafe's eyes and almost laughed aloud. What dogs-in-the-manger most men were! They didn't want you themselves, but they didn't like you admiring another man.

'I'm sure he'll be delighted to show you his collection,' he said stiffly, and after that the conversation languished.

They had reached the pre-coffee stage when Alain Savin approached their table. He greeted them both, then fixed his gaze on Sara appreciatively. 'You look charming, Mademoiselle Sara, a beautiful decoration for my dining-room.'

'*Merci, monsieur.*' Sara smiled up at him, remembering how effortlessly a Frenchman could pay a compliment, but warmed, all the same, by his pleasant manner. It was a welcome change from Rafe Jordan's surly behaviour towards her.

'I have neglected my guests, I fear.' Alain spread out his hands in apology. 'We have a new chef and I have had to keep both eyes on him. But now all is well, and I should be delighted if you would both join me for coffee in my apartment.'

Sara glanced at Rafe as he got to his feet. He didn't look particularly enthusiastic and received the invitation in silence. 'Thank you, that would be lovely, Monsieur Savin,' Sara said quickly, darting Rafe a nasty look. Why should she have to make up for his lack of manners?

'Alain, if you please,' the Frenchman smiled over his shoulder as he led the way across the dining-room. 'And I may call you Sara, may I not? I am sure we shall be friends.'

'I'm sure we shall too—Alain,' Sara murmured.

Alain had paused for a moment beside a table to speak to one of his guests, and Sara felt Rafe's hand touch her arm and was aware of his breath on her cheek as he leant down to her ear and growled, 'No need to overdo the lovey-dovey act. The client's already hooked, you know.'

She made a quick movement, shaking off his hand, glaring up at him as indignantly as she knew how, trembling inside with impotent rage. She'd like to—to . . .

With an effort she controlled her temper. Professional women, she reminded herself, should be able to resist an emotional reaction, however goaded they might be. But she couldn't help turning her back pointedly on Rafe as the three of them made their way to Alain's apartment.

To Sara's delight, the apartment was in one of the two towers she had glimpsed as they arrived at the hotel. As they climbed the curving stairway Alain gave them a potted history of the building—the original castle dated from the reign of Louis IX and had been largely dismantled in the sixteenth century, when the main part of the château was built.

'I am glad they left my tower standing,' Alain smiled, leading them into a fabulous room where the ancient stones of the rounded walls still remained, and the furnishings, rich and luxurious in jewel colours, seemed to lend a Renaissance grandeur to the place.

Alain served dark coffee in tiny fragile cups, and Sara's fascinated gaze moved around the room as she drank, thinking of the immense problems that must have confronted those early builders of massive castles and cathedrals, without the help of all the technology used in modern times. 'Such buildings make a mere architect feel very humble,' she said. 'I'm sure our efforts will hardly be still here six or seven hundred years hence, will they, Rafe?' Go on, she willed him, say something. Don't just sit there looking like a thundercloud! He had only contributed monosyllables to the conversation since Alain had joined them.

Rafe directed a smile that wasn't a smile towards her. 'I'm sure *yours* will, Sara.'

'Bravo! Gallantly spoken!' Alain beamed, utterly missing the sarcasm that ran below the words. 'Sara has great talent, that I am sure of. Her design for my gallery was most intriguing—quite different from the rest of the designs you were kind enough to show me, Rafe. All of them were highly—competent, you understand, but Sara's had that something extra. I myself would call it—*heart*. It seemed that she understood my need to build it as a memorial to my wife.'

He looked admiringly towards Sara, who felt herself flush at this rather fulsome praise. Rafe wasn't going to like *that*.

Obviously he didn't. After a few more minutes he put down his coffee-cup and got to his feet. 'You'll excuse me, I'm sure, Alain, I have a quantity of paperwork to get through. You and Sara can have a preliminary discussion about choosing a site for the gallery. Perhaps tomorrow morning we can all go out and take a look at the terrain. I'll wish you goodnight, Alain, and thank you for an excellent dinner.'

When he had gone Alain poured second cups of coffee for himself and Sara, and settled back in one of the deep crimson velvet lounge chairs. 'My poor friend, Rafe,' he sighed. 'He has been going through a difficult time, I know. I sympathise with him—although my own loss is so different. To lose a beloved wife . . .' he closed his eyes '. . . that is indeed almost too much pain to be borne.'

'I am so sorry,' Sara said gently. 'Was it very recent?' She guessed that Alain might welcome the question and not feel embarrassed by it. After Daddy had died some of his friends had been very awkward with their condolences and one or two had, she knew, actually avoided her. She had realised that it was only because of embarrassment—that they hadn't known what to say. But she had longed to tell them, 'Please let's talk about him—that would help—it's what I need.'

Alain's brown eyes—eyes that reminded her of a

devoted spaniel—met hers sadly. 'More than six months,' he told her, shaking his grizzled head. 'It gets no easier.'

'Tell me about her,' Sara invited. 'She must have been a lovely, interesting person, to want to collect beautiful things.'

A tiny smile pulled at the Frenchman's mouth. 'Lovely—interesting—yes, my Marguerite was that, and many other things too. We had a marriage—how do you say it in English?—made in heaven. We talked, we argued, we travelled together—we understood each other as if we were one person instead of two. And we made love—ah, yes——' An expression of great tenderness passed over his face and he shook his head. 'Never would I want to marry again, you understand. I prefer to have my memories. And my work, of course.' He brightened up a little.

'Your hotel? It's quite superb,' Sara told him sincerely. 'I knew only Paris and the parts just outside when I lived here with my father, who was an artist. I hadn't realised that the Loire valley was so beautiful.'

'The most beautiful part of France, I believe, but of course I am biased. But tell me about your father—what was his name?'

To Sara's delight it turned out that he knew of her father's reputation and had seen his work in exhibitions. And that, of course, led on to other topics. Alain told her of the first visit he and Marguerite had made to Japan and how he had started his collection of *netsukes* at that time. Proudly he showed her a display case, where rows of tiny ivory objects, carved or painted, nestled against soft black velvet.

Once started it seemed as if he couldn't stop. He talked of the travels he had taken with his wife, of the adventures they had had together, of the excitement in tracking down items for their collection. She'd been right, Sara thought, Alain Savin was a fascinating man to talk to and listen to.

But at length he looked at his watch. '*Tiens, tiens*, I had forgotten the time! Rafe will be cross with me for keeping you so long.'

Rafe, thought Sara wryly, will certainly not be cross, he'll be only too pleased to get me out of his sight for a while. But she allowed Alain to escort her back to the suite in the hotel annexe, where it became obvious that Rafe had either finished his paperwork and gone out again, or had never come back here at all. Probably the latter, she guessed. He had merely wanted to get away from her, and he would most probably be located in the bar.

Alain lingered in the hallway. 'You are comfortable here, Sara? If there is anything you need please do not hesitate to tell me.'

Sara *did* hesitate, but after only a moment she plucked up courage to say, a little uncomfortably, 'If it is possible to have locks on the bathroom doors, at least——? It would make things a little more—private, you understand?'

Alain clapped a hand to his forehead. 'How could I not think of that? I will give orders for it to be done tomorrow.'

Sara thanked him and hoped that she didn't look as relieved as she felt. Alain mustn't know that relations were miserably strained between Rafe and herself—it would give him a bad impression of the work they would be doing for him as a team. Almost better to let him believe—as he might well do—that they were sharing a bedroom as well as the bathroom. But he was much too suave and sophisticated to hint at that. Instead he wished her goodnight and told her once again how much he had enjoyed their talk, and kissed her hand with great gallantry before he retired and left her alone.

When he had gone Sara stood looking around the hall. The wisest thing to do would be to go to her own bedroom and avoid seeing Rafe Jordan again today. But she didn't feel particularly tired, and anyway she mustn't let his absence or presence dictate to her, except in a professional situation, of course.

There were two doors at the far end of the hall and she opened each in turn. The first disclosed a cloakroom, with lavatory and hand basin in the same flower-decorated ivory colour as the bathroom. For the use of visitors, presumably, and Sara felt a sense of relief. This would make the sharing of one bathroom marginally less intimate.

The second room turned out to be a modern kitchen, all in white, small but fully equipped and with the gleaming, unused look of a display in an exclusive store. Could it be that Alain had never had the thrill of bringing his wife to this beautiful apartment he had planned to share with her? Had she, perhaps, died before they could live here together? Sara's mouth suddenly twisted with pity.

She wandered around, opening cupboard doors, and found packets of tea and coffee, sugar, biscuits. In the fridge were milk, cream, and butter, also a selection of wrapped cheeses.

Marvellous! Tea was exactly what she needed. She put the kettle on to boil, found a tin of Darjeeling tea and opened a packet of milk. Cups and saucers were in another cupboard and she hesitated about putting a cup for Rafe on the tray, then decided against doing so. She wasn't going to play the 'little woman' for Rafe Jordan!

She heard the hall door open as the kettle boiled and a moment later he appeared in the kitchen doorway.

'So you *have* come back?' He leaned his head against the door frame, surveying her under lowered lids. 'I looked in half an hour ago, but you weren't here, and I thought perhaps Alain had persuaded you to stay—to comfort him in his sad loss.'

Sara's eyes widened with shock and anger, her hand shook violently, and the steam from the kettle scalded her fingers. She held her hand under the cold tap, wincing with the pain.

'Did I score a hit?' Rafe's voice mocked her. 'I take it you declined the invitation?'

Sara drew in a deep breath. Then she pulled a paper towel from the roll and wrapped it carefully round her fingers. No emotion, she told herself, simply look him straight in the eye and say what you have to say.

'I'm afraid,' she said, standing up very straight, 'that it was a mistake for me to come here. I would suggest that I return to London tomorrow and that one of the others—Bob Stratton, perhaps—flies out to take my place. Frankly I find your attitude insulting and offensive, Mr Jordan, and I'm not prepared to go on working with you.'

That was that, she thought, and if it costs me my job,

so be it.

She hadn't had time to imagine what his reply would be. Vaguely she had thought he would jump at her proposal to leave. That seemed to be the reason for his behaviour—to make it impossible for her to stay in the firm. She certainly wasn't prepared for the rage that sent the colour from his cheeks, leaving them ashen beneath the healthy tan. He crossed the kitchen and gripped her shoulders. 'You mustn't go,' he rasped. 'You can't.'

'Of course I can,' Sara said, keeping her voice calm. How she managed it she didn't know, for her heart was thumping inside her like a road drill and her legs were trembling violently.

His fingers were biting into the flesh of her shoulders under her thin dress. She could feel his anger as if it were a swirling red mist surrounding her.

Then, suddenly, it all changed. 'Oh, Sara—Sara——' he groaned. 'You've got it all wrong.' His hands left her shoulders and passed down her bare arms. They encircled her waist and pulled her close against him, pressing his cheek hard against hers. 'Oh, God,' he muttered, 'I never thought it would happen again—not like this.'

There was desperation in the way he held her body against his, and in the way his mouth met hers in a long, hard kiss. She could feel his heart thudding against her and her own heartbeat quickening to match his. She mustn't respond to him—she mustn't. She'd only known the man a few days, and it was painful and humiliating to feel the way her body was slowly taking fire.

It was a totally new sensation, nothing like the feelings she had had from her tentative explorations into sex during her university years. A delicious weakness was spreading over her lower limbs and at the same time a sharp erotic desire quivered between her thighs. She heard herself moan as she felt the tense masculine hardness press against her softness. She began to lose all sense of time, of everything except the erotic sensations that were awakening inside her. Her arms went round his waist pulling him closer—closer . . .

His kiss deepened, becoming more demanding as he felt her response. 'Darling—darling——' His voice was anguished as he lifted her in his arms and carried her into the bedroom and lowered her on to the big bed. 'Can we—please——?' he pleaded.

From some remote part of her mind came the message, clear as a bell. *You can't—you mustn't—it's all wrong. It isn't you he wants, it's another woman.*

He was kneeling beside her on the bed, his fingers fumbling with the front fastening of her dress. He hadn't touched her body yet. She ached for the feel of his hands on her breast, and yet instinctively she knew that if she let him go further she wouldn't be able to stop. 'No,' she gasped, dragging his hand away. 'No—no—*no!*' The last word came out in a muffled scream, and she rolled over and lay with her back to him, her hand pressed to her mouth. There was a long, strained silence. Then she felt him move away from her. She pulled herself up in the bed and saw that he had sunk into one of the tapestry-covered chairs and was sitting very still, his head lowered into his hands, his fingers threaded in his dark hair.

Sara stood up groggily, pulling her dress down over her knees. She leaned against the bed for a moment, one hand to her forehead. She'd been doing something when all this started—what was it? Then she remembered the steaming kettle. Of course, she'd been making tea when Rafe came in.

Leaving him sitting there, she stumbled into the kitchen and found a pool of water on the worktop and a pot of tea with the lid off. Automatically she wiped up the spill and emptied the pot down the waste-disposal. She tried to think, but her brain felt like sawdust. Where do we go next? she wondered, but no answer presented itself, except that the situation must be cleared up—*now*.

Rafe came into the kitchen. He had evidently put his head under the cold tap, for his dark hair gleamed wetly in the overhead strip lighting.

He stood in the middle of the kitchen, surveying her with a dark, brooding look that made her inside shake. 'Thank you for stopping me making a fool of myself,' he said. 'I should have learned better by now, but apparently I haven't. I'm sorry I started that——' he jerked his head towards the bedroom '——but you couldn't have been altogether surprised, after what happened in the car. You must have realised . . .'

'I don't realise anything,' Sara snapped. He wasn't going to blame her for what had happened, surely? 'All I know is that you've treated me in a most extraordinary way since you first set eyes on me in the office. I put up with it as long as I could, but when I had the nerve to ask why, you took advantage of our being in the car to—to . . .'

'I kissed you—yes,' he put in. And to her amazement he smiled.

It was the first time he had smiled at her without a

cynical twist to his lips or a sarcastic sneer, and the smile sent a jolt through her like a thunderbolt. Suddenly the whole room went into a spin before her eyes. She leaned back against the worktop and for a dizzy moment she thought she was going to faint. With a great effort she concentrated on his next words. '... and very pleasant it was too,' Rafe was saying, 'as also was our joint performance a short time ago. I got the impression that you might be enjoying it too.'

Sara felt the heat rise into her cheeks. 'You're the expert,' she mumbled, fighting to keep her voice steady. 'You've had a lot of practice, of course. You know all the techniques.'

The smile disappeared abruptly. 'Quite.' He bit the word off.

He came closer to her and put one hand on the worktop. Sara stood her ground, resisting the urge to move away. He hadn't taken his eyes from her for a moment since he came into the kitchen, and now there was a grim look on his face that made her mouth go dry with alarm. Was he going to send her back to London? Had he decided that there was no place for a woman on a job like this?

He said tersely, 'It must be fairly obvious to you that I find you a threat to my peace of mind, Sara. I shall just have to work on my self-control, because the very last thing I want is to get involved with you—in spite of some evidence to the contrary,' he added, his lip twisting. 'No doubt it will get easier when we start on the job tomorrow. So I propose we concentrate on that and put the matter of any personal relationship behind us.'

Relief flooded through her. It would have been a

horrid blow to her confidence if her first important assignment had ended in failure. That was the only reason she wanted to stay, wasn't it? *Wasn't it?*

'That suits me,' she said stiffly. '*I* certainly don't wish to get involved with *you*. But I doubt if I can work with you if you go on being so—so—aggressive. Being irritable now and again is one thing, and understandable, but deliberate hostility is quite another.'

'All that——' He waved a hand dismissively. 'Merely a defence mechanism. Ignore it.'

Ignore it, he says! Calmly—just like that! Sara had to bite her lip to stop an angry retort bursting out. If she wanted to stay on in France and continue with this fascinating work she had to accept Rafe's company on the terms he set out. That, she reminded herself, was professionalism. Because she was a woman he would no doubt expect her to be emotional and resentful—which she had been until now, she had to admit. Most men would have taken Rafe's barbed words with a shrug and ignored them—as he suggested.

She'd show him, she vowed. From now on, she would be cool, impersonal, entirely professional.

Just—her heart gave a little throb as she made herself meet his dark, sombre eyes—just so long as he didn't touch her again!

CHAPTER FOUR

SARA expected to lie awake all night in the big four-poster bed. It had been quite a day, what with the journey and all that came after, and her head was teeming with confused impressions, all of them concerned with Rafe Jordan. For a little while she tried to put them into some sort of order. She wished she knew more about him—for instance, what traumatic experience he had had with his ex-wife to explain why he had become so bitter about women, and especially women with red hair! It would have been funny if it hadn't been so painful.

He might be bitter, but he was also a very passionate man, that was certain. Her inside squirmed as she remembered his lovemaking. He'd been almost out of control then, and if she hadn't stopped him he would most probably be lying here beside her now, their arms entwined, their legs . . .

Her heart began to thump violently and she sat up and drew in several long breaths. She mustn't start fantasising about the man. All right, he was dangerously attractive, but he wasn't for her. Not for a night, not for a week, not for anything less than a committed relationship, and that he was surely not going to offer her—red hair or not.

She lay down again and made herself picture Alain's gallery. Alain was such a dear man. She remembered how he had confided in her, how he had shown her his treasured collection. Now, if only Rafe could behave like a civilised human being the three of them could work so happily together. Damn, there she was thinking about Rafe Jordan again. She must think about the work they were going to do together, not about the man himself. Perhaps, as he said, things would be better tomorrow, when they started to choose a site and make a preliminary survey.

Perhaps she would be able to forget the feel of his arms around her, the hard demand of his mouth—perhaps——

There was an odd little smile on her lips as she drifted off to sleep.

Sara wakened to daylight shining round the edges of the blue velvet curtains and to a loud knock on the door. 'Come in,' she called sleepily, vaguely aware that she was staying in a hotel and that this would be a maid knocking at the door. The door burst open and Rafe appeared. He was wearing a short burgundy silk robe and carrying a tray and his dark hair was rumpled. Sara pulled herself up, blinking at him stupidly.

'Good morning, Sara, I hope you like morning tea,' he said briskly, 'because I've brought you some.' He put the tray down on the bedside table, poured out tea for them both and sat down on the edge of the bed. 'And how is my pretty colleague this morning? Sleep well?'

'Very well, thank you.' Sara was conscious that her flimsy white nightdress showed all of her arms, most of her shoulders, and that the oval, frilled neckline was decidedly on the low side for entertaining men in her bedroom.

But Rafe scarcely glanced at her as he sipped his tea. It was easy to guess that he had been thinking things over and that this morning he was demonstrating that he was well in control.

'This is the scenario for the day,' he told her. 'We breakfast here in our apartment—no, I'm not asking you to cook, the waiter will do the needful. He will also bring us a luncheon basket which we shall take down to the proposed site by the lake—which is quite a distance from the hotel itself, through the wood. A very thoughtful idea of Alain's, he didn't want to put us to the fag of coming back here and having to pretty ourselves up for lunch in the dining-room, after scrambling about in the wild wood all morning.'

Sara grinned. 'Scrambling about in the wild wood—sounds fun!'

'It's work, not fun.' He scowled at her with mock-ferocity. 'I shall be a hard taskmaster, so prepare yourself, my girl.'

Sara sipped her tea. 'I'm prepared,' she said meekly. 'But work can be fun—*should* be in a perfect world, where everyone does the work he or she loves best.'

'Hm.' Rafe looked unconvinced. 'Been reading William Morris, have you? But anyway, it's too early in the morning for such deep thoughts.' He stood up and put his cup on the tray. 'You have another cup of tea while I take a shower. I'll bang on the door when I've finished.'

'OK.' Sara felt curiously happy all of a sudden. She could like Rafe Jordan in this mood. Things might not be so difficult after all. She looked out of the window and said, 'It's a lovely morning, and I insist on having fun. Will Alain be coming with us? He said something last night about . . .'

'No, he won't.' Rafe's face hardened as he cut in. 'Problems with the new chef, apparently.' He turned towards the bathroom door. 'I'm afraid you'll have to put up with me. Too bad! I *do* apologise.'

The hateful sarcasm was back in his voice again. Sara stiffened. There was no reply to that, and she watched the tall, straight back as he disappeared though the doorway, a small frown creasing her forehead. If they had been friends, he might have meant that playfully, but they weren't, and he hadn't. It didn't take much to make him revert to his earlier nasty, needling remarks, did it? She supposed it had become a habit. 'Merely a defence mechanism,' he'd told her. 'Ignore it.'

Sara sighed as she slid out of bed. She'd have to try to ignore it, because evidently there was no way she could avoid putting him on the defensive. It had seemed a harmless enough remark—to ask if Alain would be coming with them. Why should he have resorted to sarcasm, almost as if he were—jealous? Sara slid back the door of the big closet and took out her flimsy cover-up. He couldn't be jealous of *her*, so it must have been some sort of reminder of past hurts. Very bad past hurts. He wasn't going to tell her, of course, why should he?—She was only a girl who worked in his department. Nothing intimate about their relationship. But a few minutes ago she had thought they might get closer—even become friends.

She sighed again, rummaging in her bag for clean bra and panties. The prospect of fun seemed to have gone out of the day.

But three-quarters of an hour later, as they left the hotel by the big front entrance, her spirits rose again.

'It's a fabulous place,' she said, pausing to look back at the hotel. Last evening, looming up out of the dusk, the château had seemed a little formidable, the scene of some Gothic tragedy perhaps, but this morning, as sunlight bathed the twin towers and the intricate stone structure to either side of them, and glinted off the rows of windows, it presented a softer picture. 'It must be full of history.'

Beside her, Rafe moved impatiently. 'Probably. You can ask your friend Alain about it—I'm sure he'll be delighted to give you all the details.' He moved on purposefully, carrying the luncheon basket in one hand and a black leather portfolio in the other. Sara supposed he had all the instruments they would use. He hadn't instructed her to bring anything herself, but she had taken the precaution of tucking a clipboard and pencil under her arm in case it was needed.

She hurried after Rafe along paved paths across smooth lawns with flowerbeds, past an inviting-looking swimming pool, its turquoise waters ringed by marble surrounds on which blue-striped canvas loungers were arranged in carefully casual groups. She was glad she had popped a swimsuit in her bag at the last minute, just in case! Surely there would be an opportunity for a swim? Or was Rafe going to keep her tied to work every moment of the day?

She eyed his straight back as he strode ahead of her and thought that probably he was. He was wearing navy shorts today and a thin shirt to match, and his long, muscular legs were deeply tanned. He moved easily, swinging along at a great rate, and she had almost to run to keep up with him. That would most likely be the story of their stay here, Sara thought, her spirits sinking a little. He would be calling the tune and she would be very much the junior member of the team.

Beyond the lawns the hotel grounds became wilder. Paths disappeared, and the shrubs had been allowed to grow thickly, competing for space. Further on, the shrubbery gave way to a wood of feathery low-growing trees. Sunshine pierced the canopy of quivering leaves, throwing changing patterns of light and shade on the soft ground beneath.

Sara broke into a run to catch up with Rafe. 'This is wonderful, just as I imagined it,' she gasped. She couldn't contain her delight.

He stopped and looked down at her, dark eyes narrowed. For perhaps half a minute he studied her face. Then he said, 'Your eyes look greener under the leaves. Or else it's a trick of the light. You're a walking traffic signal, my girl—green eyes, red hair. Green says go, red says stop.'

Sara laughed. Suddenly she felt happy again, careless of what she said. She pointed to the cream-coloured knitted top she was wearing over her jeans. 'Amber says proceed with caution.' She was flirting with him, but he had started it. Now he'll probably put me down with some horrid snub, she thought, but strangely, she didn't care.

But he didn't. He said, 'I'll bear that in mind.' Then, to her confusion, and without releasing the basket or the portfolio he was carrying, he leaned towards her and kissed her on the mouth lingeringly. Then he turned and walked on ahead.

Sara's knees felt like elastic and her breathing was erratic. Oh, lord, she thought, what's happening to me? She was a mess—a mixture of anger that the man seemed to be taking her for granted, kissing her just when he felt like it, and a kind of horrified knowledge that she enjoyed it far too much. With a resolution that she would never, never, never again rise to any bait he carelessly threw out, she padded after him, stumbling a little on the thick carpet of leaf-mould underfoot.

Presently the trees thinned out and there, before her, the photograph she had worked from became reality. Sara caught her breath, staring, because it was all exactly as she had pictured it. Here was the small lake, irregularly shaped, the far side overhung by dipping trees, small inlets to right and left disappearing mysteriously into the woods behind. Immediately in front of her was a narrow strip of shore where tiny waves turned over each other lazily as a breeze ruffled the greenish-brown water of the lake. On the left, at the far end of the shoreline a wooden gazebo was built so close to the lake that tall reeds flapped gently against its low windows.

Rafe made for the gazebo and put down the luncheon basket on the bench inside. 'This is the kind of site you had in mind?' He opened the black leather case, took out Sara's drawing and spread it out on the circular wooden table in the middle of the small building.

'Yes—oh yes, it's marvellously right. I do hope it works out. This is such a heavenly place.'

'Well, we shall just have to see, shan't we?' he said drily, and she wished she had phrased it differently. He wouldn't appreciate her romantic enthusiasm. It would be all very practical from now on—she must remember that.

Rafe glanced towards the lake. 'The probable depth of the water table bothers me rather. We won't want to get involved in a lot of expensive drainage operations.'

'No, of course not,' Sara said hastily. 'The shore slopes quite steeply; perhaps we could get enough depth of dry footing if we sited the building some way back.'

After that technicalities took over. Sara's drawing was subjected to a minute analysis and at first she began to wonder if anything would be left of her original idea. But she couldn't help admiring Rafe's lightning-quick brain. Not even the tiniest point escaped his notice. 'That wouldn't work,' he kept on saying, 'But we can get round it like this. Look, Sara . . .' His pencil flew over the paper, sketching in alterations that would solve the difficulties while altering the plan as little as possible.

When he finally straightened his back and put his gold pencil down Sara felt as if she'd been put through her final examinations all over again. She sat on the bench and pushed her hair away from her face. 'And I thought I'd been so clever,' she admitted.

'Oh, you were—you are. You've done very well.' He sat down beside her and glanced at her under dark lashes. 'You didn't think I was getting at you, in my own inimitable fashion, did you, by suggesting alterations to your plan? I wouldn't sink as low as that, you know.'

'No,' Sara said calmly, 'I didn't think that. Your father told me before I left that you weren't in the best of moods just now, but that I'd find you co-operative and helpful to work with.'

He laughed. 'Good old Dad! The soul of tact as usual! It's a good thing he didn't tell you what I said to him on the phone.'

'I can imagine. You'd rather any of the others had been accepted. You must have been really furious when Alain chose my drawing.'

He seemed to be turning that over in his mind.

'Furious? No, that's not the right word. I was—let's say—apprehensive. But let's not dwell on that now. Let's have lunch. I'll clear this stuff up.' He took the plans from the table and replaced them in the portfolio.

Sara opened the luncheon basket, and surveyed the contents with unashamed greed. 'Super! My mouth's watering. They've even provided a tablecloth.' She spread the red and white check cloth on the table. 'Now we can pretend we're in Montmartre.'

'You lived in Paris at some time?' Rafe helped her to set out the food— a selection of cheeses, pâté, a long *baguette*, luscious white peaches, a bottle of red wine.

Sara broke the *baguette* in half and tore off a hunk. She nodded. 'Traditional artist's studio. My father was an artist, you see.'

'Ah—yes, I do see.' Rafe regarded her with interest. The only seating in the gazebo was the wooden bench beside the table, which meant that they were sitting side by side, and much too close together for Sara's composure. She was horribly conscious of the muscular thighs showing below the navy-blue shorts and was thankful that she had chosen to wear jeans herself—otherwise their skins would be touching if they both moved at the same time.

Rafe, however, seemed unconscious of her closeness—or at least unaffected by it—and he tucked into his lunch with zest, at the same time shooting questions at her about her father's work and her life in Paris.

'So,' he said, as he dealt neatly with opening the bottle of red wine without which no French lunch was complete, 'you gave up your dream of becoming an artist and settled for the next best thing—architecture. Am I right?'

Sara blinked in amazement. 'How did you know?'

He smiled with maddening superiority. 'An inspired guess! I think I'm beginning to understand you a little, Sara. And of course your drawing for the gallery was as much art as architecture.'

'Oh!' She pursed her lips. 'I don't think I like that remark. And there wasn't any next-best-thing about it. I think architecture *is* an art. Surely you do too?'

He nodded. 'Certainly. Don't look so fierce, my child. I wasn't denigrating your work. I've seen the beautiful working drawings you've been turning out back in London. You're doing fine.' He put a pacifying hand on her knee.

'Don't!' She winced away from his touch before she could remind herself that he was merely being friendly.

He looked down at his hand with a grimace and removed it. 'Perhaps you're right,' he said wryly. He examined the space inside the gazebo. 'The accommodation in here is a little—er—intimate. I wouldn't like to strain my self-control too far. Or yours,' he added.

Sara felt her face flame. '*My* self-control is in perfect working order.'

'Oh, yes?' The dark brows went up. 'Well, we won't argue about that. Have some wine?'

He filled her glass without waiting for an answer and went on, 'So—your father was an artist, and you lost him fairly recently, I understand. Is your mother still alive?'

'As far as I know,' Sara said stiffly. 'We don't communicate.'

He had his ironical expression again as he said, 'The child of a broken marriage? Poor Sara!'

'I can live with it,' she said hardily. 'Being on one's own has its compensations. You can please yourself what you do.'

Rafe nodded. 'My own sentiments exactly. I'm glad we're agreed on that point—it sets my mind a little more at rest.'

Sara drank her wine. She probably should have refused it—she wasn't accustomed to drinking wine at lunchtime—but the day was hot and the wine wasn't a heavy variety. She wasn't in danger of getting tiddly, but she had a pleasant feeling that she could hold her own with Rafe in this converation.

She looked him staight in the eye. 'Seriously,' she said. 'You don't really believe that the colour of my hair poses any threat to you, surely?'

He leaned back against the rough wood of the wall behind him and surveyed her thoughtfully over the rim of his glass. For what seemed ages he didn't speak and his scrutiny moved from the top of her head down over the soft curve of her breast under its thin cream-coloured cotton top, to where her legs were tucked under the table. Then they returned to her face. By now her heart was thumping erratically and she looked away from him, her cheeks hot. Why on earth had she risked asking what was palpably a leading question?

The silence lengthened unbearably. At last she ventured a glance at him and saw that his face was expressionless. 'The answer,' he said, 'is yes.'

Sara winced inwardly. Fool, she berated herself. Idiot—to invite a snub like that! Just when things had seemed to be getting on a more friendly footing between them. Whatever it was about her—or the colour of her hair—that brought out the worst in him, he wasn't going to tell her.

She stood up and began clumsily to put the remainder of the lunch back in the basket. 'Shall we . . .' she began.

She had intended to say, 'Shall we get back to work?' But, to her surprise, his hand went out and grasped her wrist and pulled her down beside him.

He said, 'Did you ever wander round museums when you were a child? I did, and I remember very well that there were charming iron contraptions called man-traps. Have you ever seen one? No? Well, they're not pretty things. The gamekeepers of the lords and squires used to set them to catch poachers. The poor devils would walk into one in the undergrowth and—snap!—it caught him by the leg. Some of them even had teeth that tore the flesh and . . .'

'Don't!' Sara shuddered, and tried to draw her wrist away, but his fingers didn't relax their hold.

'Sorry, I got carried away. I was just thinking that the man-woman attraction is like that. You walk into the trap and before you know it you're caught tight.'

'I don't see what all this has to do with me,' Sara said, which wasn't altogether true. She knew quite well what he was getting at and she didn't like it at all.

He put out his other hand and touched her hair. '*You're* a man-trap, Sara. Only fortunately I've seen you in time.'

She jerked her hand again and this time she managed to get it free. 'You're offensive!' she spluttered. 'Insulting——'

He shook his head slowly. 'I'm paying you a compliment, actually. Man-traps aren't conscious of their lethal power, and neither, my child, are you. Or so I'd judge. The fault, if there is one, is in me.' His face was suddenly drained; he looked so infinitely weary that Sara's hurt feelings were forgotten. Ridiculously, she wanted to put her arms round him and comfort him.

She pulled herself together rapidly. 'I think we should get back to work,' she said.

He smiled faintly. 'Well said, Sara. Keep it up and perhaps we shall weather the storm.'

What an extraordinary way of putting it, Sara thought, as they left the gazebo and walked back into the wood. As if a storm was already gathering and would presently engulf them. That wasn't going to happen—how could it when they were both determined to avoid it? Rafe certainly was—he'd made no secret of it—and she had to place her trust in the good sense that had protected her until now in her dealings with the opposite sex. She couldn't deny his physical attraction or her own response to it. But forewarned is forearmed, she told herself, and she had no intention or entering into a casual affair with Rafe Jordan.

For most of the afternoon they explored the terrain behind the lake, selecting possible sites, returning to the gazebo to stand poring over the plan that Rafe was roughing out. Between them they had put together a rough map, showing the location of all the trees, the distance from the lake and the compass bearings, and indicating the position of the entrance door leading to the passage which, in turn, would lead to the main gallery.

'It's coming together splendidly.' Sara stood looking over his shoulder as he drew the plan. 'I can *see* the main door there among the trees. You would come on it unexpectedly, like a lovely surprise. It would be . . .' She broke off. She really mustn't let herself use flowery language; she didn't want to give Rafe the chance to be ironic about her romantic approach to her job. She must remember she was a professional architect, as he was.

But suddenly she was terribly aware that she had leaned too close and her face was only inches from his glossy dark hair. She gazed at it, fascinated, seeing the way it curled into his sunburnt neck, smelling the clean, astringent smell of the lotion he used on it, and she was helpless to stop the churning that started inside her.

'Would be what?' he said softly, turning his face up towards her before she could manage to draw back. 'Magic, were you going to say?'

Sara swallowed and touched her tongue against her dry lips. 'Something like that,' she muttered.

His eyes held hers, their dark, liquid depths stirring depths inside herself that she had been unaware of until this moment. Then, without looking away, he nodded his head slightly. 'Magic,' he said slowly, as if he were trying out the word to see if it fitted. '*Black* magic, perhaps.'

For what seemed ages their gazes locked together and Sara felt a slow warmth stealing up her body. Rafe drew in a ragged breath and she could see a pulse beating in his throat. 'Damn you, Sara Bennett!' he growled.

Abruptly he got to his feet, sweeping the papers from the table into the black portfolio. 'As it's not considered safe to plunge into the lake I propose to go back to the swimming pool—which might be cold enough to reduce my temperature. You can please yourself,' he added brusquely, and walked out of the gazebo and away through the trees, pushing aside the branches as if they were enemies bent on hindering his progress.

Sara stood where he had left her, then sank down on to the wooden bench and let out a long breath. This wasn't going to work, was it? Rafe seemed unable to come to terms with having her here purely as a colleague. Something about her—the colour of her hair, presumably—turned him on, and it seemed likely to happen, out of the blue, at any moment. She wasn't aware of actually saying or doing anything provocative—that retort about the amber colour of her top had been pure fooling, and anyway, he had started it. So why had he sworn at her just now as if she had deliberately set out to tease him? Was it going to be impossible for them to work together? And would that mean that she would have to give up the job she valued so much? No, she thought, somehow I'll make it work. I'll make him believe that I'm not a threat to his peace of mind.

Slowly Sara gathered up handbag and clipboard, and began to make her way through the trees back to the hotel. After a minute or two she heard the pad of feet approaching on the soft ground and the swish of branches being pushed back. Her heart gave a lurch. Rafe come back? To say he was sorry for his abrupt departure? No, surely not—that wasn't Rafe Jordan's style.

A moment later the branches parted in front of her and Alain appeared. His handsome face broke into a charming smile as he saw her. 'Sara—Rafe told me I'd find you somewhere around here. He had to go in to finish off some drawings and I thought I'd like to get an idea of how the plans are going on.'

'Oh *yes!*' Relieved, Sara returned his smile enthusiastically. 'I'd love to show you. We've done great work today and really come up with a few ideas.'

She turned back and led the way through the trees to a small clearing. 'We thought we could site the main door here. How would you like a crystal glass door which would sparkle when the light fell on it through the leaves?'

'Ah, yes, good! I like that. And I can add a suggestion. I have an old friend who lives near Chinon who is a wizard with glass. He does the most beautiful engraving work. I think you and Rafe should go and have a talk with him about the door, yes? We will arrange it. Now, beyond the door—what?'

Sara spread out her arms, indicating the way the building would take shape behind the main door. 'And then the passage would go along here, perhaps gradually widening out into the main gallery——' She marched on ahead, explaining the way it might be, seeing the building as if it already existed, the sun shining through the trees on to the mellow stonework. 'Rafe thought we might be able to build in stone, in the same way as the hotel extension was done. What do you think, Alain?'

The Frenchman was watching her face, her green eyes shining with enthusiasm, a tinge of colour in her pale cheeks under the aureole of Titian hair. 'I think it will be very beautiful,' he said quietly, 'as would anything you designed, little Sara. You are so beautiful yourself that you could surely not make anything ugly.'

She felt herself flush. 'Oh,' she said uncertainly. 'Oh well, thank you very much.' Then she laughed to dispel the faint embarrassment that had crept into the conversation. 'That sounds hopeful for my success, doesn't it? May I apply to you for a recommendation?'

'Assuredly you may,' he told her gravely. 'I have many friends around here and I will tell them all that there is a beautiful, talented young lady architect who will design them exquisite houses and——'

'Stop!' Sara held up her hands. 'Don't forget I already have a job in London. A very lowly job, really, with Rafe Jordan's firm. It was pure luck that you should happen to like my drawing and that I should come out here to meet you.'

Alain gave a little bow. 'I am lucky too. And Rafe is lucky to have such a talented assistant. I'm sure he knows it.' Sara thought he was eyeing her a little curiously. Had he already guessed that everything was not exactly harmonious between herself and Rafe?

They began to walk back together through the wood. Alain said suddenly, 'I have had locks put on the doors in your apartment, as you wished, Sara. It was very remiss of me not to think of it before. You see, those rooms are never used in the ordinary way. But as the hotel is full just now it seemed a good idea to offer you and Rafe the apartment as living and working quarters. They were designed, as Rafe may have told you, for my wife and me, but we never occupied them. There wasn't time.' His voice was sad.

'They're beautiful rooms,' Sara said quietly, 'and they'll be perfect to work in. Please don't think I was complaining—I just wanted the locks because—because . . .' She broke off awkwardly. What could she say that wouldn't sound either naïve or give Alain a false impression of Rafe's approach to her? 'I wouldn't like you to th-think——' she stammered.

Alain put a hand at her elbow and gave it a

reassuring squeeze as they emerged from the wood and came out on to the lawn beside the swimming pool, where guests were lounging and sunbathing on the canvas day-beds. 'No need to explain,' he said suavely. 'I do not think anything—anything at all.' They stopped beside the pool. 'You like to swim, Sara?' Alain enquired. 'Please use the pool at any time.'

'Thank you, I——' Suddenly she stiffened as she saw Rafe climbing out of the water at the end of the pool. He wore very short black swimming trunks and his body looked magnificent, muscular and gleaming wet, his dark hair plastered down on his well-shaped head. He picked up a towel and draped it round his neck, then he saw Sara and Alain and came towards them over the grass.

Sara looked away as he joined them. The sight of the man's almost naked body was sending agitated messages along her nerves. He was so big, so—so overpowering. She glanced back and met the dark eyes fixed on her, gleaming with what looked like anger.

'I decided to have a swim before I went in to work,' he was saying to Alain. 'I can recommend your pool, my friend. The water is exactly the right temperature. Wouldn't you like a swim, Sara, to cool you off before we start work again?'

Such an innocent remark, but to Sara the underlying meaning was perfectly obvious. He knew, the brute, that their minds had been moving along parallel channels back there in the gazebo.

She gave him a melting look. 'How thoughtful of you to suggest it, Rafe, but I think I'll put off the pleasure until later. I'm keen to get on with the schematic plans on the lines we've agreed.'

Rafe shrugged and looked at Alain. 'Such enthusiasm! I wish all our junior staff were as dedicated as that.'

Alain's hand was still at Sara's elbow and now he gave it an appreciative squeeze. 'I'm in danger of becoming too lyrical about our beautiful Sara,' he smiled, 'so I will say no more. Do not work her too hard, though, Rafe. She must have some time to enjoy a little of our local attractions. We have been talking about a glass door for the gallery, and I suggest that the two of you go to see a friend of mine who is a gifted glass engraver. Sara will tell you about it, but now I must leave you and return to my kitchen, where there is much to be attended to. We will all meet after dinner again, yes?' He walked away briskly towards the hotel entrance.

Sara turned from Rafe and hurried away in the same direction. The sight of the man, fresh from his swim, was distinctly unnerving, and she hoped he would plunge back into the water and give her time to reach the apartment and her own room before he decided to return himself.

No such luck! She was only too aware that he was following close behind her, and they reached the door of the apartment at the same moment. Before she could open the door, a bare brown arm snaked round in front of her and turned the handle. She entered quickly and went straight into her room, but again Rafe was close behind her. Her arm was taken in a hard grip and she was spun round to face him.

'Why all the hurry?' he asked silkily. 'Not shy, are you, Sara? You should have elected to come out in your bikini—I'm sure you've brought one with you—then we could have met on equal terms and had a friendly swim together. There's no real urgency to start work on the drawings this afternoon, you know. Tomorrow will do just as well.'

His hand still held her tightly and she fixed her eyes on his chest with its fuzz of dark hair. She felt an alarming urge to lean nearer and rub her cheek against it. She drew away quickly. 'Please let me go,' she muttered unevenly.

Instead of complying Rafe reached out and grasped her other arm, turning her back to face him again. 'Look at me, Sara,' he said huskily.

Mutinously she raised her head and met his eyes. There was no anger in their dark liquid depths now, only a stark, undisguised hunger. 'The cold water treatment wasn't all that successful,' he said wryly. 'As you must be aware.' He drew her briefly against him and Sara's cheeks flamed as she experienced the proof of what he said.

Suddenly he pushed her roughly away from him. 'Oh, hell!' he groaned. 'I don't know what the answer is, but somehow I'm going to find one. Somehow I'm going to beat this insanity. Just keep away from me until I pull myself together.'

He turned to the bathroom that lay between their two bedrooms and stopped abruptly, staring down at the gleaming new steel lock that had been fixed on the door. 'Where did this come from? Did *you* ask for locks to be put on the doors?'

He whirled round on her, and at the sudden anger in his voice Sara felt her throat tighten, but she managed to meet his accusing eyes. 'Yes,' she said coolly, 'I did.' She wasn't going into explanations at this moment.

'Worrying about your honour, Sara, is that it?' All

the old sarcasm was back in his voice, the tone she hated. But it was more than sarcasm now, there was an edge of violence to it. He was furious.

She had no defence against his aggression. She turned her back and stood stiffly, not deigning to reply. She wanted his near-naked body out of her sight before she gave in to a sudden urge to make physical contact with him, to lash out at him with her fists, to wipe the sneer from his handsome mouth. He hadn't moved, and she clenched her hands, waiting for him to go. Instead she felt him come up behind her, felt his arms clasp her in a steely grip just below her breasts, felt the heat of his breath on her cheek as he leaned near.

'Well, if you've decided to treat me like a wild animal, to be kept behind locked doors . . .' his voice was dangerously soft in her ear '. . .I shall take that as an invitation to start behaving like one.'

CHAPTER FIVE

SARA stood very still, her heart starting to race. Rafe's hands gripped her tensely, then loosened, moved up a little; she felt their warmth and vitality through her thin cotton top. A wild animal, he said! He didn't mean that seriously, she thought, feeling a wave of sensuous languor stealing over her as his hands moved slowly, rhythmically on her breasts. It had only been his usual irony.

His hands found their way under her cotton top, dealt expertly with the front fastening of her bra. She should stop him, but the sensations he was arousing seemed to drain her of energy. The bra was undone now and her breasts were released into his hands. His fingers brushed gently over the sensitive peaks and Sara felt them rise and harden, and stifled the moan that rose in her throat.

She should stop this before it went any further, a warning voice sounded at the back of her mind. But the pleasure he was giving her was so blissful . . . so intoxicating . . . seeping through her body like strong wine. She stood motionless, trying to resist an urgent need to lean back against him, to press herself against his hard, muscular strength. Then, his hands still on her breasts, his mouth nuzzled her hair away at the back of her neck and as she felt the pressure of his lips on the sensitive curve there, her resistance crumbled. She relaxed against him, feeling the warmth, the hardness of the man, and a sharp thrill pierced through her as their bodies met.

But at the same moment she felt fear. What was she doing, allowing this to happen, and how was it going to end? Was this the way of a wild animal playing with its prey before the final assault? And didn't they say that the hapless quarry actually enjoyed the moment of surrender? But she wasn't going to surrender, she wasn't going to . . .

'Oh, God, Sara, what you do to me!' muttered Rafe, and he twisted her round roughly and lowered his mouth to hers. His kiss was different, this time, from his other kisses. There was a new intensity, a new urgency about it as his tongue eagerly prised her lips apart and entered her mouth, hungrily probing the moist depths.

His lifted his head away for a moment. 'You're enjoying this, aren't you, my darling? You want it just as much as I do?' he murmured unsteadily.

His eyes were too close to hers to focus on clearly. They were like a dark sea, mysterious, hypnotic almost. She was drowning in them and she didn't care. She heard herself murmur, 'Yes . . . oh, yes . . .'

Then everything changed. Things were happening over which she had no control. She was being urged towards the bed, lowered on to it. Rafe was beside her, breathing in rough gasps, and his hands were everywhere, hurting, bruising.

She knew that he was losing control, and panic hit her. She had never encountered the wild, primitive male desire that had him in its grip now. She could feel the heavy throb of his heart as her body was clamped against his and his breath came quickly and raggedly, close above her head.

'No!' she gasped, pushing at him as he lowered his

damp body over her. 'No—I don't want . . .'

'But I do,' he muttered harshly. 'I want very much . . .' Then his mouth was fastened on hers, greedily demanding, as one hand grabbed the cotton top and dragged it over her head, pulling her bra roughly from her shoulders so that she was naked to the waist. She heard his grunt of satisfaction as her breasts were exposed to his touch. For a moment, as she felt his mouth close over the sensitive peaks, biting and pulling, Sara was aware of a sharp wild thrill of excitement to match his own. A frantic new world of sensation was opening out before her, inviting her to enter—to enjoy—to luxuriate in . . .

He was kissing her lips again now and at the same time his hands were at the zip of her jeans, his legs thrown over hers, imprisoning them. She heard the slide of the zip open and felt him ease himself up a little to pull her jeans down. In another moment she would have gone over the brink and it would be too late. From somewhere deep inside her a certainty welled up that it shouldn't be like this the first time—it mustn't. There should be love—or if not love, then at least tenderness, not this frantic, greedy—lust.

Gathering what strength she could command, she bent her knees and pushed the heel of her sandalled foot hard down against his shin, not caring how much she hurt him. At the same time she bit sharply into his lip and tasted blood. She heard his outraged shout of pain, and then suddenly she was free and scrambling off the bed, panting with nerves and fright.

Her legs were like jelly as she grabbed her top and

stumbled across the bedroom into the small cloakroom which led off the hall. She sank on to the dressing-stool before the mirror and stared at her ashen face. She had to get out of here—and quickly. She pulled on the top and smoothed it down; the bra had got left behind. She zipped up her jeans. She splashed cold water over her hot cheeks and restored her mass of dark red hair to some sort of order. Then she opened the cloakroom door a crack and listened, hardly breathing.

There was no sound of movement from her bedroom as she slid past the door and out into the passage that led to the hotel lounge. At this time in the afternoon it was almost empty, and she crossed it quickly and went out by the side door that led into the garden. She stood looking round confusedly. She had to be alone, but where? It was a warm afternoon and there were still people lounging round the pool, people sitting at tables on the patio with their drinks, people wandering in the garden. Too many people.

She turned away from the path that led into the wood. If Rafe was going to look for her, that was the place he would look, and she couldn't face him yet. Stumbling slightly, she made her way down the lawn and through an archway that led into a rose garden and further on through another archway into a small walled garden. At any other time Sara would have been fascinated; it all looked so ancient, as if the crusted grey stones in the walls and the low bushes of fragrant herbs in the centre bed and the lichen-covered pavement had been there since the castle's beginnings.

There was a stone seat beneath an overhanging tree,

and she slumped down on to it and tried to sort things out in her mind, but the more she tried the more hopeless it seemed. The facts were clear enough: Rafe Jordan had a powerful sexual drive and there happened to be something about her that turned him on. That was all there was to it, except that he was angry and resentful about it.

The danger was that what had just happened back there in the apartment could so easily happen again, and she didn't know if she would be strong enough to resist him. She'd been teetering on the brink as it was; he'd aroused sensations in her that she'd never felt before. She almost wished now that she had experimented with sex when she was at college, as most of the other girls had. But Sara had a fastidious dislike of the casual pairing-off that went on at parties, the hot, fumbling hands and wet mouths, the calm assumption that she would be ready and eager to disappear into a bedroom, or into a thicket of bushes with some stranger she hardly knew. After one or two distasteful episodes she had stopped going to parties, and fairly soon it had been taken for granted that Sara Bennett was narrow-minded and provincial and she was left alone. She hadn't minded. All the more time to devote to her work. One day, she promised herself, she would meet her man—and then she would *know*.

But now she wished she were more experienced, more able to cope with a man like Rafe Jordan. She felt hopelessly out of her depth with him. The one thing she was resolved on was that she wasn't going to allow anything to interfere with the work here. It was her big chance and she wouldn't give it up. If Rafe Jordan found her presence disturbing then that was his problem—let him deal with it.

That seemed simple, didn't it? She wished she didn't have this feeling that it wasn't all that simple. She'd left her own emotions out of the reckoning. She leaned over and picked a sprig of lavender from the bush that was spilling out of the centre bed, sniffing its fragrance idly. How *did* she feel about Rafe? It would be easy to say she hated him—hated his sarcasm, his masculine arrogance, his easy assumption of superiority. And yet . . . that was all a defence, he had said. A defence against her and her attraction for him.

No, she didn't hate him. At least—sometimes she hated him and sometimes she . . . her thoughts stopped dead and she realised she was crushing the lavender flowers between her finger and thumb. It couldn't be that she was falling in love with him, could it? That would be a pretty silly thing to do, Sara, so you mustn't even contemplate it, she told herself. The sun was going down now and the summer afternoon was getting chilly. She must have been sitting here longer than she knew, but the thought of going in and facing Rafe was daunting. She leaned against the back of the seat, closing her eyes, trying to relax the nagging tension in her head.

Then her eyes shot open. Rafe was standing in the archway leading from the rose garden. He looked groomed and very much in command of himself, in jeans and a cream shirt, dark hair gleaming from a shower—cold? Sara guessed, trying to extract a vestige of humour from the situation.

'So this is where you've got to.' His face was grim. 'Running away, were you?'

Sara swallowed. 'I suppose you could call it that.'

He nodded and came and sat down on the opposite end of the stone seat. 'Things got a bit fraught in there, didn't they?'

Sara's green eyes flashed with indignation. A bit fraught—was that all he was going to say? When he'd very nearly raped her, when he'd behaved like a—like a frenzied animal, leaping on her like that! She compressed her lips in silence.

'I suppose,' he said, 'you're expecting an apology, but I'm not very good at apologising and you probably wouldn't believe me if I said I was sorry. Anyway, the blame wasn't all mine, if blame has to be handed out.'

'You're blaming *me*?' Sara fumed. The arrogance of the man! 'I most certainly didn't——'

'Oh, yes, you did. You said "yes" at first and then changed it to "no". A man likes to know where he is.'

Sara was silent. It was true, she thought miserably. That was exactly what she had done.

'We won't argue about that now, though, we have to decide what has to be done,' Rafe went on quite calmly. He might, she thought, have been attending a board meeting. 'First of all, I'll have to ask Alain to find me another room—we certainly can't go on sharing the apartment. I suppose he thought he was doing us a good turn by putting us there together. I'll have to convince him otherwise.'

'Try explaining your man-trap theory to him,' Sara suggested nastily. 'Unless, of course, you think it would put you in a bad light to seem so vulnerable.'

'But I *am* vulnerable, damn it!' he shouted. Then, more calmly, 'If we go on sharing that apartment, the next thing will be we'll be sharing that very comfortable bed. And then—because you're a "nice girl", not a girl for short-term flings . . .' He stopped, looking hard at her under those long curving lashes. 'You're not, are you?'

'No,' she said firmly. 'I'm not.' Of course she wasn't. But when she looked at his brown, supple fingers as they rested on his knees, a glint of gold at his wrist where he strapped his watch, when she smelled the faintly astringent dressing he used on his hair, when she lifted her eyes to meet the dark eyes under frowning thick brows, she had a quickly suppressed wish that she *were*.

He shrugged. 'You see? The next thing looming up would be marriage. And that . . .' he slammed his fist on the seat between them '. . . is definitely not on.'

'All right, all right, you've made your point. No need to shout,' said Sara. 'I really can't see why you're making this great fuss about it. Plenty of men have a failed marriage behind them, and they don't reject the female sex for that reason.'

'Oh, I don't reject all your sex—not by any means,' Rafe said hatefully. 'Only the "nice girls" like you, Sara. The ones who have "permanent commitment" written all over them.'

Sara looked at him. 'I wouldn't like to say what I see written all over you, Mr Jordan,' she said. Then, with cool curiosity, she added, 'Don't you ever intend to marry again?'

'No!' he roared.

'But surely—one failed marriage . . .'

'One failed marriage—and I don't intend to make it two.'

'And what makes you think I'd be interested in

marrying you?' she said coldly. 'I promise you I wouldn't, Mr Jordan. You're perfectly safe with me. I don't intend to marry for some years yet, and anyway . . .'

He was looking at her so strangely that the words died on her lips. 'Don't you, Sara?' he said softly. 'Don't you really? I see it differently. When I look at you I seem to see us standing in front of a registrar and vowing to love and cherish each other for the rest of our lives. I know myself, I know what kind of girl you are. And I see the marriage-trap opening again.'

Sara had ground the sprig of lavender to powder and she tossed it aside, getting jerkily to her feet. 'I'm not prepared to sit here and listen to . . .' Her throat choked up humiliatingly.

Rafe reached across and gripped her arm, pushing her down on to the seat again. Then he released her arm as if her flesh had stung him. 'You're going to listen,' he said. 'I'm going to make you see.'

His eyes were fixed on her with deadly seriousness now. Sara waited, watching his face with its closed-up, defeated look, and had a twinge of sympathy for him, which she quickly suppressed. The last thing he would want from her would be sympathy.

He looked away from her, fixing his gaze moodily on the tumble of bushy herbs in the centre bed. 'I married young—too young, actually. She—Denise—was exquisite. Smooth white skin, great grey eyes, adorable mouth.'

He hesitated. 'A tumble of dark red hair.' He turned to Sara and she saw his hand move as if it would touch her own hair. Then it fell back to his knee.

'I was besotted with her,' he went on more quickly.

'She was nineteen—the daughter of one of my mother's friends. My parents had a wonderful marriage and I was brought up in a warm, loving family. I took it for granted that my own marriage would turn out like that. A home—children—a beautiful wife waiting for me in the evening. You know—"Little Grey Home in the West" stuff. Well, it didn't turn out like that. Oh, at first it was wonderful—there was the whole fascinating world of sex to explore together. And Denise had quite a circle of friends. She was lively, vivacious, the centre of everything, and I was bursting with love and pride because she was mine. But after a year or so it became evident that I was neglecting the job in my father's firm—the job I was just starting out on. I had to spend more time away from home, had sometimes to let Denise down when she'd arranged dinner parties, had to tell her I couldn't always spare time for theatres, trips abroad . . .'

He shook his head impatiently. 'Oh, the old, old story, you've heard it so often. The disappointments, the quarrels, the accusations, the gradual drifting apart. Denise got in with a new circle of friends, including older men, richer and much more important than I was, and sophisticated women that I didn't care for at all. Then . . .' he paused briefly '. . . then Denise found she was pregnant. I was over the moon. I thought she'd settle down at last. I almost went out and bought a teddy bear and a cricket bat! I started to dream again of a house full of kids, a welcoming wife—all the old stuff. But she didn't see it that way. She insisted that she was too young to start a family, we should wait for a few years. One of her smart women friends knew of a good place . . .'

'Oh, no!' Sara gasped, appalled.

'Oh, yes,' Rafe said flatly. 'You can, perhaps, imagine my reaction.'

She nodded, shivering slightly. She could imagine it only too well—she had already seen fury on his face.

Rafe was silent for so long that Sara thought he had forgotten her. Then he said slowly, 'I came home one night and found there wasn't going to be any baby.'

He drew in a harsh breath. 'I suppose that was virtually the end. For a while, after I'd got over the shock, I tried to patch things up. You see, I loved her, I tried to look at it from her point of view. I still hoped things would get better somehow. Then, one day, she said there was another man and she wanted a divorce. I refused point-blank. She was my wife and I wasn't going to let another man have her. I think I went a little mad that night.'

His smile was a grimace. 'It wasn't exactly rape, you understand, there was still something there between us. But Denise chose to believe it was. Afterwards she packed a bag and went to the other man. He was a property developer—a millionaire three or four times over. Denise always liked money.' He shrugged. 'End of the marriage. That was five years ago.'

The silence stretched out again.

'Well, that's that,' he said at last, straightening up. 'Now you know the lot, and I've absolutely no intention of repeating the performance. You probably can't understand why I feel so—threatened, but I assure you that seeing you, being with you, is a constant threat.' He stared down at her, black eyes brooding.

'It isn't just sex, Sara. I know I want you—I've made that only too plain—but I could so easily persuade myself that I'm falling in love with you. I recognise the symptoms. And I'm absolutely determined that I won't let it happen.

'So . . .' He stood up. 'This is how it's going to be. You and I will be alone together as little as possible from now on. You can push ahead with the drawings. I shall be away looking up the contractors—we'll use the same firm that worked here before. When I've got it more or less on the rails I shall go back to London, find some excuse not to return here, and brief young Stratton to come out and finish the job with you. He's quite competent to do that and it will be good experience for him.'

He paused, frowning down at Sara's pale face. 'And if you think I'm running away from danger, you'll be dead right, I am,' he said. 'But let's try to see the lighter side of it. It *is* rather ridiculous, don't you agree? And there's nothing like a good laugh to defuse a potentially emotive situation. That's what I tried to get Denise to see, but I always failed dismally. Come on, Sara—smile!'

She looked up and met his eyes. They weren't smiling, although his mouth was. She felt cold all through, cold and numbed. Her feelings, and her pride, had taken a battering, but there was nothing to be gained from sulking. Rafe had been utterly straight with her and she supposed she should appreciate that. And if Denise lacked a sense of humour *she* certainly didn't, she thought with a spurt of triumph. Her mouth curved reluctantly into a smile and then suddenly they were laughing together.

'That's my girl,' said Rafe. 'Come along and I'll buy you a drink before dinner. Anything you fancy.'

As they walked back up the garden Sara knew that a crisis had been met and passed. Their relationship was on a different footing now. Perhaps, she thought rather bleakly, they could be friends. That might be better than nothing.

The following days passed exactly as Rafe had sketched out. Sara had the annexe apartment to herself, except for the times when Rafe joined her in the sitting-room, which had assumed the character of an office. A large drawing-table had been installed, together with all the paper and instruments she needed to work on the next stage of the project—the series of schematic design sketches which would be presented to Alain for his approval.

There were two site conferences, attended by the structural engineers and cost consultants—firms which had been employed previously. Sara was always carefully included in every detail of the work—Rafe was meticulous about that. He introduced her as 'my colleague, Mademoiselle Bennett', and she was accepted as one of the team. This, she persuaded herself, was what she wanted. The personal involvement with Rafe Jordan had been a terrible mistake, and she tried to welcome the way he spoke to her, looked at her, as if she were simply a business acquaintance with whom he got along quite well. Which was, she assured herself frequently, exactly what she was.

There were no breakfasts together in the apartment. Sara's breakfast was brought in by a waiter and she ate it alone. Ditto her lunch, except when she was at a conference. Rafe looked in occasionally to supervise the work she was doing and expressed himself entirely satisfied with it. Sometimes she wondered if he would notice a mistake if she'd made one. He certainly didn't examine the drawings very carefully. No more leaning over her desk, so that their heads were together, as had happened in the gazebo. Just a hearty, 'Good work, Sara, keep it up,' and he was gone, leaving her curiously unsatisfied and depressed.

They met for dinner at their small corner table in the large, ornate dining-room, but the meal took the form of a business meeting. There was plenty to discuss about the work, and personalities were never once touched upon. After dinner they took coffee in Alain's private apartment, so that they could talk over the plans and report progress.

Alain was as courteous and affable as ever, but sometimes Sara caught him turning a puzzled look on her. She wondered what Rafe had told him about their relationship and she began to feel awkward and self-conscious at these evening meetings. Usually she excused herself when the business of the day seemed to be over, and went off early to bed.

After six days the first stage of the project was finished. Rafe had gathered together a team of consultants, Alain had approved the detailed design for the gallery and it was time to move into the development of working drawings and specifications.

On Friday afternoon Rafe looked in at the sitting-room-cum-office while Sara was packing up for the day. 'I've decided to leave for London this evening—

in about half an hour. I'll be staying in Paris overnight,' he told her abruptly. 'Everything's on target and the next thing is to get on with working drawings and specifications. François will keep in touch——' François was the manager of the construction company '——and you can phone him if you're in doubt about anything. When I get back to London I'll put Bob Stratton in the picture and I'll let you know when he'll be arriving. OK?'

Sara couldn't look at him. 'OK,' she said. Her mouth was suddenly dry and her hand shook as she replaced her working instruments in their velvet-lined case. A pair of dividers slithered from her fingers and dropped to the floor, and she bent to pick it up at the same moment that Rafe did. Her hair brushed his cheek and he started away as if he had been stung.

'Sorry,' she said mechanically, and was humiliated to hear the stiff resentment in her voice. She wouldn't want him to know she was hurt by his rejection.

She looked up and he was standing staring down at her, his face grim. It seemed to Sara that everything that had been left unsaid between them for six whole days suddenly rose to the surface and clamoured to be spoken.

Somehow she forced a smile to her lips. 'Have a good trip,' she said fatuously.

She saw his hands clench and knew he was angry. Well, what did it matter? What did it matter that he said nothing—just turned on his heel and walked out of the room?

Quick tears blurred Sara's eyes. The trouble was, she thought miserably, that it *did* matter. It mattered so much that she felt as if he had cut her into small pieces and left them lying quivering on the floor behind him. Against all common sense and all her instincts for survival she was deeply, painfully in love with him.

CHAPTER SIX

IT should have been easier for Sara, knowing that Rafe had left for London, but it wasn't. She couldn't get him out of her mind—even when she was concentrating on her work he was there, looking over her shoulder. She could feel his breath on her cheek, smell the healthy, male smell of him, hear his deep voice as he made alterations to and suggestions about the plan.

She wanted him with her, she ached inside for the sight of him, the touch of his hand. And when the job here was over and she returned to London, then what? She didn't dare think ahead as far as that. Perhaps she would have got over this obsession by then. You *did* fall out of love, everyone said so. You woke up one morning and found you didn't care any more. But it hadn't happened for Rafe, had it? And just now that seemed a very remote possibility for her.

Sara dined alone at the corner table in the dining-room each evening. Usually Alain stopped to have a word with her, as he did with several of his other guests, but there was no invitation to take coffee in his apartment, and anyway Sara wouldn't have accepted. She was aware of a certain constraint in his manner towards her, although he was as charming as ever.

She worked as usual on Saturday and Sunday, only breaking off to take a quick dip in the pool. Beyond a smile and a word she had had no communication with any of the other guests, and that suited her. She was in no mood for making holiday acquaintances.

On Monday morning Alain rang her on the internal telephone just as she was preparing for work.

'Good morning, Sara, how are you? I have missed our evening talks.'

'I'm fine,' she lied, thinking of how she had tossed and turned in the big bed until her travelling clock said half-past three.

'*Bon, bon.* Well then, I have a suggestion to put to you about the glass door for the gallery. You remember I told you that I knew a man who was an expert glass engraver? I would very much like to take you to see him in his workshop. What do you say, would you like to go?' He sounded tentative, almost shy—if you could imagine Alain being shy.

'Yes, thank you, I'd love to.' It would be a relief to get away from this place where everything reminded her of Rafe.

'*Bon,*' he said again, pleased. 'It is about an hour's drive. I could get away about ten and we shall have lunch at a small inn I know of, near Chinon. It will be most enjoyable.'

Enjoyable! Sara wondered if she would ever be in the mood to enjoy anything ever again, but strangely enough she found she *was* enjoying herself as Alain drove her in his large, comfortable saloon car along the leafy country road that followed the Loire Valley.

He seemed in high good humour and intent on giving her a good time. He took on himself the role of guide, pointing out places of interest as they went.

'This part of France,' he told her 'is called the château country, because there are so many beautiful châteaux here—all along the banks of the river. Some are almost ruins, some have been restored and are now hotels—as my own hotel is—and some are tourist attractions. The Château de Chenonceaux is one—it is *magnifique*. I wish there was time to take you there; perhaps you would like to see it another day? I like to think of the past there—of the court life with festivals and masquerades, of the elegant men and exquisite women in their silks and satins and jewels.' Alain sighed. 'I fear I am a romantic at heart.' He gave Sara a rueful glance.

Chinon itself seemed to Sara like a reminder of the Middle Ages. The castle, Alain told her, was one of the oldest in France, made up of three separate fortresses, each separated by a deep moat. 'Here is where our Joan of Arc met the Dauphin and managed to put some backbone into him,' he chuckled. 'That's how the story goes—maybe Joan was the first of the feminists.'

Sara grinned. 'You disapprove of feminists, Alain?'

'Not if they are beautiful,' he said slyly. 'Are you a feminist, Sara?'

She considered the question. 'Half and half,' she said at last. 'I can't put it any more definitely than that.'

Sara found the visit to Monsieur Blanc utterly fascinating. He was a tiny man with a brown face like a nut, who wore baggy trousers and a somewhat greasy black beret. He lived and worked in a street so narrow that the tall houses seemed to be nodding to each other across the worn flagstones, casting a cold shade between. He greeted them with dignity and ushered them into his workshop, where specimens of his work, both finished and unfinished, glistened on thick wooden trestles.

Sara's French was hardly up to following the conversation between Alain and the old man. Alain knew exactly what was needed, and she left him to explain the pattern he wanted for the engraving while she moved round the cluttered workshop, admiring the delicate glass pieces with their intricate patterning.

She let out a little cry of delight as she saw a tiny, squat jug with a simple stylised rose engraved on it. 'Oh, I love that!' She pointed it out to Alain. 'Is it for sale, I wonder? Could you ask Monsieur Blanc?'

She pulled a face when she heard the price. 'Another time, perhaps,' she said to the old man in careful French, on her way to the door, thanking him for letting them see his work.

Alain stayed behind for a minute or two to take his leave of his friend and then joined her, folding up a piece of paper on which he had sketched the pattern of the engraving for the front door of the gallery.

'A very satisfactory visit,' Alain announced, when they had driven out of the town and arrived at the inn where he had planned to lunch. They were shown to a table in the garden beside the river, and Alain took the piece of paper from his pocket and passed it to Sara. 'This is only my amateur effort,' he said with his wry smile. 'Monsieur Blanc will make a work of art of it. It will be exactly the engraving that my Marguerite would have adored.'

A waiter came up and lunch was ordered. '*Omelette Créole*, I think,' Alain announced. 'It is a speciality here. With fruit and a local wine. Would you like that, Sara?'

'Sounds lovely,' she agreed happily. It was a sunny day and Alain was a delightful companion and she had seen something of an interesting, historical town, and her idea for a crystal glass door had been approved and set in motion. What more could she need! she asked herself, smiling at Alain across the table. 'I *am* enjoying myself,' she told him. 'It was so nice of you to ask me.'

'Nice!' He pulled a face. 'It is my great pleasure.' He looked slightly uncomfortable as he added, 'I admit I hesitated at first, after Rafe left, to approach you. I did not know exactly how things stood between the two of you. It was plain that there was something . . .' He waved his hands expressively. 'I did not wish to interfere . . .'

'Oh, Rafe wouldn't care what I did,' Sara burst out bitterly and unwisely, and saw Alain's eyes narrow. 'But don't let's talk about Rafe. Tell me some more about Monsieur Blanc—he's such a lovely old man . . .'

She listened to Alain's stories about the places he knew so well and the characters who lived in these parts, but with the mention of Rafe the atmosphere had changed subtly, and she was glad when Alain said regretfully, as they finished lunch, 'I am so sad, but we must return now. I have a new guest arriving this afternoon, and it is my custom to greet each new guest personally, you understand.'

Sara was silent on the return journey and Alain concentrated on his driving, his face thoughtful. He drove the big car straight into the garage and turned to Sara.

'I have to thank you for a most pleasant day, Sara,' he said rather formally. 'I have not enjoyed myself so much since . . .' he broke off, then hurriedly felt in his pocket and drew out a small object, wrapped in crackly brown paper. 'I hope you will accept this as a memento and an expression of my gratitude for your company and for your work on my gallery.'

Sara removed the paper to disclose the little glass

jug she had so admired in Monsieur Blanc's workshop, and her eyes misted. 'I don't know what to say,' she faltered. 'You are so kind—thank you. I'll treasure it.' She fumbled for a handkerchief and blew her nose. 'And when I'm a famous architect I'll keep it on my desk to remind me of my very first contract.'

The Frenchman's brown eyes were soft as he touched her hand gently. 'You deserve success, Sara. And happiness,' he added. 'They do not always go together, of course.'

He got out of the car and came round and opened Sara's door, and they strolled back around the side of the hotel to the forecourt, where a taxi was arriving. The driver began to unload several large travelling bags, while a small boy emerged from the back seat, and stared up at the château. He looked about four or five and he was dressed in a perfectly tailored copy of a man's suit, with a white shirt and a red bow tie. Quite the little gent! Sara thought, amused.

But there was nothing grown-up about the way he was dancing up and down with excitement, big dark eyes shining. 'Mama, come and look, it's just like the pictures in my history book!' He spoke English with a faint American accent. 'It has arrow-slits . . . do come and look . . .' He pointed up at the towers on either side of the central building.

A woman emerged gracefully from the car and proceeded to pay the driver, waving away the boy's excitement with a bored gesture.

Alain gazed at her. *'Ravissante!'* he murmured. 'Madame Franklin—the wife of a millionaire, I understand.' He gave Sara a cryptic grin before going forward to greet the newcomer.

Sara stood for a moment, watching. All the women

staying at the hotel were in the high-income bracket, no doubt of that. You only had to look at their exotic clothes, their golden bodies, their sleek hair-do's. But this woman was going to provide competition. She wore a pure white suit in a heavy silk that followed the sensuous curves of a perfect body. Even from this distance Sara could see that she was exquisitely beautiful, and very aware of it. Everything spelled it out—the way she moved, with a faint sway, the way she tilted her head as Alain approached, the languid gesture with which she held out a hand to him.

And oh, dear! Her hair, so beautifully sculptured to her head, was a rich, glossy dark red.

Rafe shouldn't have left, Sara thought, trying to see the joke. He wouldn't have bothered to look twice at me, with that gorgeous redhead in his sights.

Two women appeared from the hotel, strolling towards a car that was parked in the forecourt, their remarks reaching Sara's ears clearly.

'My dear,' the younger one crooned in English, 'did you see *that?*'

The other laughed lightly. 'You know who she is, don't you? She's Denise Franklin—the wife of Philip Franklin, the property millionaire. They say he dumps her and the child in luxury hotels while he travels around Europe. Playing the field, no doubt . . .' Their laughter drifted away on the evening breeze as they climbed into their car.

Sara stood quite still, suddenly icy cold. Denise? Could it possibly be, or was it too much of a coincidence? She remembered so clearly Rafe's words: 'He was a millionaire property developer. Denise always liked money.'

And her hair! Oh yes, it all fitted in. It had to be true.

As Sara went slowly into the hotel and straight to her bedroom thoughts were buzzing round in her head like a swarm of wasps. The one that settled and stung most painfully was the one that told her what a pathetic fool she had been to allow herself to fall in love with Rafe Jordan.

Up to now, she knew, she had let herself cherish a faint hope that he might change. A very faint hope. But now that hope was quite, quite dead. Now that she had seen for herself the woman he had loved. Perhaps still did love, for all she knew.

She picked up a strand of her own richly red hair and tugged at it viciously. 'This is all your fault,' she said aloud, and laughed a little hysterically. Then the laughter turned to choking sobs, and for the first time since her father had died Sara wept long and bitterly.

An hour later she was showered and dressed in a simple leaf-green dress, one of the dresses she had bought for the trip—reminding herself that she was coming here to do a job, not to compete with the wealthy guests—and ready to go into the dining-room for dinner. Competent make-up had disguised the fact that her eyelids were swollen. Eye-drops had brought a green glitter to her eyes. Her hair was brushed to a silky mass that curved into her neck.

When she managed to stop crying she had talked very seriously to herself and reminded herself that she was a budding architect, a young woman of nearly twenty-five, enjoying her first success. She might have missed out on adolescent love affairs. She might be reaping the reward for being hopelessly inexperienced where men were concerned. But that didn't mean that she need make up for it by falling for the first man who had the skill to awaken her dormant eroticism.

She stood in front of the long mirror, smoothing down the softly pleated silky green skirt of her dress, assuring herself that she looked just what she was—a self-assured young professional woman. Fixing a faint, slightly bored smile on her mouth, Sara made for the almost empty dining-room.

The small corner table was a good vantage point to see everyone who entered the room. Sara smiled at the waiter, who by now was an old friend, and gave her order, trying not to look as if she were waiting with an uncomfortably quickened heartbeat for a certain eye-catching red-haired woman to come in.

Diners drifted in slowly, in small parties, or in couples. Tables filled, waiters moved around noiselessly, the buzz of conversation began to rise and fall. The smell of exotic food hung temptingly on the air.

Sara concentrated on her *foie gras frais de canard* and scolded herself for allowing her nerves to get the better of her again. What did it matter if the vision she had seen getting out of the taxi was indeed Rafe's ex-wife and long-lost love? If he'd been here things would have been different, but he wasn't here and wasn't going to return, so no awkward situation was likely to arise. And anyway, she told herself sternly, Rafe Jordan's marriage disaster had nothing whatever to do with her.

Then, when she had almost finished dinner, Denise Franklin made her entrance, Alain by her side. As she glided to the table he indicated Sara noted with amusement that a few seconds' hush fell on the room, and that the men's eyes slewed away momentarily from their partners.

Sara couldn't resist taking a look across the room. Yes, this Denise was gorgeous, one had to admit that. Every inch of her spoke of beauty parlours, health farms, top fashion salons—the pampered life of a very rich woman—chic, manicured, elegant. She wore a black dress of some clinging matt material that proclaimed Paris, and her only jewellery was a pair of huge gold hoop earrings studded with diamonds, that reached almost to her shoulders. Her rich red hair was softly curled and pinned up on to the crown, allowing a few stray wisps to curl round her ears with studied artlessness. Had she looked like that when she was married to Rafe? *If* she had been married to Rafe. But of course the whole thing might be one huge coincidence. Coincidences happen all the time, Sara assured herself as she applied herself to her favourite *gâteau de Pithiviers,* a marzipan-flavoured tart that was one of the new chef's specialities.

She decided that she would not take coffee at her table; she would make it herself in the apartment. It was stupid, she knew, to feel threatened by this Denise Franklin, nevertheless, she did. Two redheads among a company of not more than twenty guests was one too many; that was how she put it to herself, but deep down she knew there was more to it than that. Deep down there was an uneasiness that she couldn't quite explain.

She got to her feet, intending to slip round the side of the dining-room and out through the side door, from where she could make her way to the entrance lounge and from there to her apartment. But as soon as she stood up she saw Alain coming across the dining-room to her.

He smiled his charming smile. 'You have enjoyed

the meal, Sara, yes?'

'Delicious,' Sara told him. 'Your new chef is a wizard, Alain.'

He nodded. 'You must meet Jacques and tell him so, Sara. He will be enchanted. But now there is something I have to ask you. My new guest, Madame Franklin, is anxious to make your acquaintance.'

Sara's green eyes widened. '*My* acquaintance—but I don't want . . .'

He moved closer and went on in a low voice, 'She tells me that she had heard that Rafe was working here and she very much wanted to meet him. There is, it seems, something of particular importance she wants to speak to him about. She asked when he would return, and I had to admit that I did not know exactly.'

He pulled a contrite face. 'I am afraid, Sara, that I was, perhaps, tactless in telling her that you might give her the information she requires.'

'Oh!' Sara's hand closed tightly over the smooth back rail of her chair. So it was true! She thought now that she had known all along. 'I'm afraid I can't tell her much about Rafe's movements or . . .'

Alain said hastily, 'Of course not—but just have a word with her, would you, Sara, to help me?' He wrinkled his nose comically. 'Madame Franklin is a very persistent lady indeed.'

Sara sighed. 'For your sake, then, Alain,' she said and, straightening her back and lifting her chin, she allowed him to lead her across the room.

Seen close to, Denise Franklin was just as perfect as she had seemed from a distance. *Ravissante,* Alain had said, and she really was ravishing. Sara told herself that she must be honest and admit that this was the kind of woman to turn men crazy. What chance did anyone have against such blinding beauty? And what chance would she have herself?

When Alain had made the introductions and disappeared towards his kitchen, Denise gave Sara a winning smile and waved a hand towards the vacant chair opposite.

'Do sit down, Miss Bennett. It's good of you to talk to me. Monsieur Savin has perhaps told you my little difficulty.' She passed the tip of her tongue over lips delicately outlined in petal-pink lipstick. How extraordinary—the lovely Denise was nervous.

Sara sat down and waited. She wasn't going to give anything away—let the other woman lead the conversation.

'You see...' Denise Franklin went on, charmingly apologetic '... I wouldn't have dreamed of troubling you, but when I heard that you were working for Rafe Jordan here...'

'Working *with* Mr Jordan,' Sara put in quietly. She wasn't going to be patronised as a kind of lower-grade secretary. 'Mr Jordan and I have been designing a building for Monsieur Savin together.'

'Yes, of course—I'm sorry. I didn't mean...' Denise Franklin touched a hand to her forehead and her rings glittered in the light from the crystal chandeliers. 'You must forgive me, I'm rather at a loss. I expected to find Rafe—Mr Jordan—here, and now Monsieur Savin tells me he has returned to London. I wonder—would you tell me when you expect him back?' She leaned slightly towards Sara across the table.

That was easy. 'I don't expect him back, Mrs Franklin. From what he told me before he left he doesn't intend to return.'

'Not coming back? Not at all?' The huge grey eyes that Rafe had talked about opened wide in dismay.

Sara shrugged. 'That's what he said.'

Suddenly Denise Franklin's manner changed. Her pink lips tightened peevishly. 'Damn,' she muttered. 'I want to see him—I must see him. I'll just have to . . .' Small white teeth closed over her lower lip.

Sara was on her feet. 'If there's nothing else I can do for you, Mrs Franklin?' she offered politely.

The other woman glanced up at her vaguely and Sara thought she had forgotten she was there. 'No—nothing. Nothing at all.' She waved her away with an irritable gesture.

Not even a thank-you! The woman really was rattled—why? What did she want with Rafe? Sara sighed as she went slowly back to the apartment and put the coffee machine on. She wasn't likely to know. Unless, of course, the beautiful Denise had split from her present husband and had some idea of getting Rafe back. Just the thought of that made Sara ache somewhere behind her ribs.

The filter machine began to bubble and she carried a tray into the sitting-room, and sat down at her drawing-table. She would do an extra hour's work before she went to bed. She had found that concentrating on work was the only way to get her emotions under control. Use your head, Sara, not your stupid heart, she told herself, and picked up a ruler.

The telephone buzzed, and her stupid heart ignored the instruction and began to bang away frenziedly. Alain, she told herself as she went across the room, it would be Alain. But before she raised the receiver some sixth sense told her it wasn't Alain. 'Hello?' she whispered.

'Sara? Are you all right, you sound as if you've caught a cold. You're not ailing, are you?'

Rafe's deep voice sounded exactly the same on the phone—it was just as if he were here beside her. Sara's knees felt very odd and she sat down suddenly. 'No, I'm not ailing.' Not unless a fractured heart could be called ailing. 'I'm fine. I was just going to start some work before I turned in.'

'Still the little workhorse?' She could see the familiar twist of his lips. His lips—oh, God, she thought. 'If you say so,' she said.

'Well, what's the news?'

'News?' she said confusedly. All she could think of was a very beautiful woman who had said, 'I want to see him—I must see him.'

'How's the work going?'

'The work?' Of course—the work. 'Oh, fine, fine. I'm getting on top of things. François has been on the phone a couple of times—he's sending his surveyor out tomorrow to do some exploratory drilling. And we've fixed up about the glass door—Alain took me to Chinon today to see the old man who does the glass engraving.'

'To Chinon?' Rafe's tone sounded wooden, almost annoyed.

'Yes, we had a lovely time,' Sara prattled on with awful brightness. 'Chinon's a fascinating town. Alain knows the history of the place and he made it all come to life marvellously. The old man who does the engraving is a character—he does really exquisite work. Alain bought me a beautiful little glass jug to commemorate the occasion and we had a super lunch at an inn by the river . . .'

She stopped. The silence from the other end of the

line was deafening. 'Hello—are you still there?'

'I'm still here,' he said. 'I'm glad you're finding time to enjoy yourself.'

Wretch! He couldn't even speak decently to her on the telephone. She swallowed, trying to moisten her dry throat. 'When are you arranging for Bob to join me?'

'It's a trifle complicated; I'll let you know. Well, if there isn't any more news . . .'

Now was the moment. Should she say, 'Your ex-wife Denise has turned up and she's panting to see you'? No, she was darned if she would. It wasn't her business; let them sort things out for themselves. Denise must know where he worked. If she wanted to see him she would have to go to London. And anyway, she—Sara—wasn't supposed to know that Denise *was* his ex-wife, was she? 'No, no more news,' she said.

'Goodbye then, Sara.'

She wasn't sure if she said goodbye. Her throat seemed to have closed up completely. She replaced the receiver with hands that shook so much that she had three attempts to get it back on its cradle.

After that there was no point in trying to do any of the fine, detailed drawing work tonight; her hands weren't steady enough. She drank her coffee standing up and then let herself out through the side door of the apartment which led straight into the garden. It was quite dark now, but the light from the dining-room spread out in a white arc across the grass, beyond which the lawns were inky black. It was soothing walking here alone, with the evening smells of growing things rising into the cool air. Sara looked up at the rugged pile of the old château against the sky, which was still streaked faintly with lemon and the smoky grey of sunset. A romantic place, she thought, a place for lovers. Oh, Rafe, why can't I get you out of my mind? Out of my heart?

'Sara?' Alain's voice came from behind. 'I thought I saw you out here.' He came up beside her. 'You are lightly clad—you must not catch cold.'

She almost laughed. Someone else anxious about her catching cold! 'I'm beautifully warm,' she said as he fell into step beside her. 'I couldn't stay indoors, it's such a lovely evening.' That was as good an excuse as any.

Alain was smoking a small cigar. The tip glowed red in the darkness. 'You managed to satisfy our Madame Franklin, I take it?'

'Not very much to her liking, I'm afraid. She wanted to know when Rafe was coming back. I had to tell her he wasn't.'

'Oh?' The little word seemed to hold a great number of questions. Sara had to decide quickly whether to leave the topic alone or pursue it. The temptation to talk about Rafe—just to say his name—was too much for her.

'Didn't he tell you—Rafe decided to send one of the other members of his firm out to work with me on the next stage of the project.'

'No,' said Alain, and she thought she heard a touch of annoyance in his voice. 'He certainly didn't tell me. I think he ought to have done. I expected that he would be returning himself.'

Sara bit her lip. 'I'm sorry—I shouldn't have . . .'

'*Non, non*, do not blame yourself, Sara. It is only that . . .' he paused as if undecided whether to go on. Then he said, 'I—do not quite understand what there is between the two of you. I imagined from the way Rafe spoke of you before you arrived that you and he were—very good friends. That is why I decided that you would like to share the apartment. But it seems I made a bad *gaffe*. I must ask you to forgive me,' he finished rather formally.

'Oh, please don't . . .' Sara put a hand on his arm and he covered it with his. There was something friendly and comforting about the pressure of his hand and she had a sudden urge to confide in him.

'It isn't quite as simple as that,' she said. 'I can't imagine why Rafe gave you that impression, because he didn't want me to come. I . . .' she gave an unsteady little laugh '. . . I remind him of his ex-wife, you see, and it makes him angry. I'm sure he's still in love with her.' Now that she had said it she felt sure it was the truth. 'It's perhaps just as well that he isn't coming back—now that Madame Franklin has arrived.'

Alain stopped walking. 'You are saying—*she* is Rafe's ex-wife? And that is why she is so anxious to meet him? *Mon Dieu!*'

'I'm only guessing,' Sara said hastily. 'I just have a hunch, from the way he described her to me—her name, and the colour of her hair—and she is so very beautiful—and she wants to see him . . .'

'Beautiful—and cold,' Alain added disdainfully. 'He is well rid of her.'

Sara laughed shakily. 'I don't think he would agree with you. But let's not talk about her any more—or about Rafe.'

'*Certainement*,' he agreed at once. 'I very much prefer to talk about you, Sara. Tell me about yourself—where you live in London—the books you like to read, the pictures you like to look at, the music you like to listen to ...'

They strolled in the garden until the light faded completely and the stars came out. A cool breeze came from somewhere and ruffled Sara's hair.

'It is getting cold, we must go in,' said Alain as they turned back towards the hotel. Just before they reached the circle of light from the windows he stopped and put a hand on her arm. 'I find you a delight to talk to, Sara. It is almost—*almost*—as if I had my Marguerite back again. She was an English girl too, you know. Well, perhaps not such a girl.' He laughed sadly, shaking his head. 'You know, Sara—if you were twenty years older or I were twenty years younger—who knows?'

Yes, Sara thought, who knows? Alain was such a dear, and he reminded her sometimes of her father—gentle, humorous, understanding. Alain was the kind of man she should have fallen in love with. Instead of which... *No, no, no,* she wouldn't keep on thinking of Rafe. The very thought of him twisted her stomach agonisingly. She smiled up at Alain and linked her arm, with his in a friendly fashion as they went back into the hotel.

The following morning Sara was up early and out at the site beside the lake, waiting for François, the contractor, to turn up with the surveyor and his team. Upon his findings the success of her plan would depend. If there wasn't enough depth of dry ground to put in footings for the main gallery then the whole idea might have to be rethought. She sighed with relief when they arrived at last. If it was going to be bad news she would rather know straight away.

François, with whom Sara had already talked on the

phone, was a big, burly man—a man of few words, and Sara couldn't help wondering if he was sceptical about having to work with a girl. But he was polite as he introduced her to the surveyors, and Sara settled down to watch while the men worked with their drilling equipment, moving from one place to another, stopping each time for lengthy conferences between themselves.

It seemed to be taking so long, she thought uneasily. She wanted to ask them how things were going, but thought better of it. She turned and looked away, across the lake, holding down her impatience.

Suddenly a small voice behind her said, 'What are those men doing?' and Sara spun round to see the little boy who had arrived with Denise Franklin yesterday regarding her gravely.

She smiled down at him. She got on well with little boys; her landlady in Winchester had had twin sons about the age of this boy and there had been tears shed on both sides when she'd left for London.

'They're looking for water,' she told him.

'Why do they want water?' Large dark eyes questioned her.

'Well, they don't want it, really. They want to be sure there isn't too much water there, where they're drilling.'

'Why?' came the inevitable question.

Sara sank down on to the grass beside him so that their eyes were on a level. 'Because,' she told him seriously, 'if there's too much water we shan't be able to make our building there.'

He thought it over and apparently gave it up. 'What's your name?' he asked.

'Sara. What's yours?'

'Philip John Franklin,' he told her. 'But you can call me Flip if you like. My daddy calls me Flip, only my mama doesn't like it. She calls me Philip.'

'Where is your mama?' Sara asked him. 'Does she know you're such a long way from the hotel?'

He shook his head. 'She's in bed. She told me to play on the lawn, but there wasn't anyone to play with.' His mouth drooped.

'Well, hadn't you better go back now?' said Sara. 'Your mama will be worrying about you.'

'Can't I stay here with you and watch the men look for water? Please let me,' he pleaded. 'Mama won't know. She's always ages and ages getting dressed.'

Sara concealed a smile. She could well believe that. No pulling on jeans and a top and running a comb through her hair for Mrs Denise Franklin!

'All right, you can stay for a while,' she said, and saw a lovely smile break out on the small, serious face. 'How old are you, Flip?'

He told her he was four and a half and his home was in Boston, Massachusetts, and he was going to start school next year. Yes, he wanted to go to school. He would have a special friend then, he added rather wistfully.

A lonely little boy, Sara thought, and wondered how much time his beautiful mother spared for him. It was ironic, she thought, that Denise had given her second husband the child that she had denied to Rafe. She must have matured since the divorce. What a blessing it was that Rafe had left the hotel before Denise arrived. He would have felt doubly bitter if he had seen her with her son.

'Mademoiselle Bennett!' François was standing

before her and she jumped to her feet.

'Yes?' she asked eagerly. 'What news?'

'The best,' he said. 'All is satisfactory, we can proceed.'

The surveyors packed up their equipment and left. François stayed behind to make arrangements for the next stage, to request definite details he needed for the contract documents to be prepared, and to touch on possible dates to begin work.

He rolled up Sara's schematic sketches and gave them an approving pat. 'Very good, Mademoiselle Bennett. *Vous êtes très imaginative!* We shall build well, all of us.'

Sara felt a delightful glow of achievement. *Something* was going right in her life!

Flip had wandered over to the gazebo and was climbing on and off the wooden bench rather aimlessly. She went across to him, smiling broadly.

'Did the men find water?' he enquired.

'No. No, they didn't. So we can put our building there. Isn't it super?'

Perhaps he was infected by her excitement. 'Super!' he echoed, and stood up on the bench and held out his arms to her.

Sara hugged him tightly, swinging him round and round, rubbing her cheek against his dark hair before she put him down. A lump rose in her throat. He was so small and light, and there was always something touching about a young child's total dependence on the adults who cared for him.

'Will you play with me?' he pleaded.

She looked at her watch. 'Well, just for a few minutes perhaps. What do you like to play at?'

For nearly half an hour a riotous game of hide-and-seek in the trees followed, until Sara dropped on to the grass, gasping. 'You've tired me out, Flip!' Her cheeks were pink, her hair dishevelled. 'Now I must take you back to find your mama.'

Flip's lower lip stuck out. 'Do I have to?'

'Yes,' Sara said firmly. She got up, patting her hair into place and holding out her hand.

He put his hand in hers obediently enough and they made their way back through the trees to the swimming pool.

Denise was lounging on a blue-striped sunbed, her sleek golden body clad in the scantiest of bikinis, her eyes obscured by huge sunglasses, a champagne glass and a portable phone on a low table beside her. Only one thing distinguished her from the rest of the reclining bodies—her hair. A blaze of Titian red in the sunlight.

'There's Mama,' Sara said to Flip. 'Run along to her now.' She gave him a gentle push towards the sun-worshippers beside the pool. This wasn't her scene, and she shrank from encountering Denise again.

Flip hesitated, his great dark eyes fixed eagerly on Sara's face. 'Can we play again?'

'Perhaps,' she said. 'If Mama says you can. Now go along—hurry!'

She paused for a moment to make sure he reached his mother, saw her look up at him as he stood beside the sunbed. She could only guess at what passed between them, but the child's back was held stubbornly straight, and for a moment he glanced back over his shoulder towards Sara.

Sara's eyes were misty as she made her way back

to the apartment. Rafe mustn't ever see this child, she thought; it would be too cruel.

And for the first time she felt compassion for the man who had wanted a son so badly.

CHAPTER SEVEN

AT first that afternoon Sara was full of euphoria and zest for work, having had François's report. But to her annoyance, as time went on, she found her thoughts straying—to her unsatisfactory conversation with Rafe yesterday, to the appearance of the ravishing Denise, with all its implications—even to little Flip. For a professional young woman who had decided to devote herself to a career rather than domesticity it was strange that her thoughts kept coming back so often to the feel of Flip's thin little body in her arms, to the pleading look in the big dark eyes when he said, 'Can we play again?'

Stop it, Sara, you're getting soppy! Now get on with the job. She chewed the end of her pencil, staring over the top of her drawing-board at the view outside the window. From here there was no sign that you were in a hotel; the window looked out on a rock garden that fell away steeply; the plants that clung to the crevices between the rocks were dry and bleached. Alain had told her that they had had no rain for weeks.

Up to now, while she had been here, the weather had been warm and sunny but with a refreshing breeze. But now Sara noticed a change. There was a stillness in the air and a humid heat that shimmered over the grass in the distance.

Inside, the atmosphere was getting oppressive. As she tried to work, the pencil kept slipping in her fingers. She passed her handkerchief over her damp forehead. There must be an air-conditioner in the apartment, but she didn't know where it was and hesitated to enquire. She persevered for a few minutes longer and then gave it up. It was much too hot to work, she told herself, yawning. It would be lovely at the site, down by the lake in the shade of the trees. Yes, she'd allow herself an hour off, why not? She was well up to date with the work.

In the bedroom she shed jeans and top, swilled her face and arms and got into a sundress—a brief little number in Kelly green with narrow shoulder-straps and a scooped-out back that reached down to her waist. Ah, that was better! What a blessing she'd packed the dress at the last moment. She'd had it for ages and it wasn't particularly fashionable, but at least it was cool.

She met nobody as she strolled through the wood. The gazebo was shaded from the sun and she went inside and sat on the bench, her head resting back against the rough wood, her eyes closed.

It was impossible to be here and not think of Rafe. She recalled every word of that unrewarding telephone conversation yesterday. He hadn't changed a bit, she thought sadly. He was still keeping her at arm's length with that horrid irony of his. Would they ever be able to meet as friends? Fantasies of Rafe and herself passed slowly before her closed eyelids, pictures that started innocently enough. She saw them sitting in front of a log fire in some cosy winter retreat, talking, comparing views, listening to music, dancing together dreamily, both his arms holding her against his firm body. Soon the pictures became dangerously erotic as the heat closed round her, relaxing her muscles, emptying her mind. At last she drifted between waking and sleeping, her senses swimming in a delicious daydream.

'Hello, Sara.' She could almost imagine she heard his voice, impossibly loving, close to her ear.

Then her hair was moving on her neck—something warm was pressing against her skin. Terrified, she jerked up, imagining some unknown horror, her eyes wide with shock. 'Hello, Sara,' Rafe said again, removing his lips from her neck, and he was smiling—smiling in a way he had never smiled at her before.

'I . . .' she croaked. She put both hands in front of her eyes like a frightened child, then drew them away. He was still there. 'I was dreaming,' she whispered shakily.

'Of me, I hope?'

She blinked at him, still not quite awake, expecting to see the usual ironic twist to his lips. It wasn't there. He looked—different. It wasn't fair of him, she thought confusedly, taking her by surprise like this. She didn't seem able to come back to the ordinary world. He was so close beside her on the wooden bench, not actually touching but disturbingly close.

She concentrated her gaze on the thin material of his trousers, only inches away from her smooth bare thighs. Silver-grey, the material was, with a blue thread running through it. Mesmerised, her eyes followed the direction of the thread . . .

'Look at me, Sara,' he said quietly.

She hesitated, biting her lip, then raised her eyes to his, and a shudder passed through her at what she saw there.

'Oh, God, Sara!' he groaned, and took her in his arms.

The kiss was brief and fierce, as if he were putting a brand on her. Then he pulled her to her feet, his arm tightly about her, his hand warm on her bare back. 'Let's go somewhere cool, for pity's sake.' His voice was rough, urgent.

There was something deliberate about the way he led her round the side of the lake, deeper into the wood. It was as if a powerful engine had started up and nothing was going to stop it on its forward thrust. Sara knew what was going to happen and she knew she wanted it to happen. She had gone past the point of no return. A throbbing started low inside her and spread over her whole body. Love and desire fused together and she pressed herself against him as they went, her head nestling against his shoulder.

As they got further into the wood the trees became more dense so that they had to push their way through the lower branches. 'This'll do,' Rafe said abruptly. He stopped in a small clearing. Green leaves, layer upon layer, made a roof above where the sun hardly penetrated. Somewhere a bird rustled softly in the branches overhead. The unmistakable smell of eucalyptus came from trees further away, nearer the lake.

Rafe turned Sara to face him, and as she looked up into the liquid dark eyes she knew that all her love and desire was spilling out over her face. It was crazy and probably unwise, but she didn't care. Everything was crazy at this moment; the world had stopped turning on its axis and there were only the two of them, here in this green grotto.

'I came back for you, Sara,' Rafe said huskily. 'I couldn't stay away. I've thought of you, wanted you every single moment—it's been agony. Oh, my darling

Sara, is it "yes" this time?'

She lifted her mouth to his. 'Yes,' she whispered against his lips. 'Oh, yes!'

A shiver ran through him as his mouth closed over hers, his tongue thrusting, exploring. She followed his lead—how easy it was, she thought hazily—why had she worried about her lack of experience? Sex was the easiest, the most natural thing in the world. Their tongues met and moved together deliciously, and tremors of excitement curled inside her. Her head went back, her eyes closed as his mouth left hers and began a slow descent down her throat, lingering in the soft hollow of her neck. One hand pushed away the narrow shoulder-straps of her dress and moved to slide down the short zip at the back.

'Pretty dress,' Rafe muttered thickly. 'But we can do without it just now.' His hand moved lower. 'And without this too.' A wisp of silk and lace followed the dress to the ground.

Then with an impatient tug his shirt was off. 'Let me look at you, my darling.' He held her a little away and his eyes travelled slowly over her naked body. 'Lovely,' he whispered. 'I knew you'd be perfect.' He lowered his head slowly and his mouth closed over the swollen tip of her breast, his tongue caressing rhythmically until Sara cried out at the sharp pleasure that spiked through her. She wound her arms tightly round his neck, pressing him nearer, feeling the rough fuzz of hair on his chest against the soft mound of her breasts. For moments they stood locked together, just savouring the delight of contact in this magic place, with the sunshine filtering through the leaves.

Then, gently, Rafe lowered her to the ground. The leaf-mould was dry and slightly prickly, but she hardly noticed as he lay down beside her, his hands and mouth exploring every inch of her, every crevice and hollow, rousing her to a frantic need that grew more and more insistent as his fingers found new, even more sensitive parts.

He lifted himself on one elbow and looked down into her flushed, dreamy face. 'Is it possible—is this the first time for you?'

She couldn't speak, her breath choked in her throat and she could only nod and turn her face away. He wouldn't want her now, she thought with sudden numb misery. He wouldn't want an inexperienced virgin. Sophisticated men like Rafe didn't, she knew that. The fear of failure settled over her like a heavy black cloud. 'I'm—I'm sorry,' she muttered.

He put his hand under her chin and turned her flushed face towards him. '*Sorry*? Why?' His lips curved. Was there a trace of the old irony there? She couldn't be sure.

She bit her lip hard as tears flooded her eyes. This was all going horribly wrong. 'Because—because . . .' she faltered.

He laid a finger over her mouth. 'The talking stops here,' he said.

She heard the impatient whirr as he pulled down the zip of his trousers. Then they were discarded and he rolled his body on hers.

Sara's relief was exquisite. She had been so afraid, and now it was all right—it was wonderful—he didn't mind about her ignorance. Confidence returned and she relaxed beneath him, moving sensuously to his rhythm, her hands stroking his broad back. She wanted him so much, she had never known this gnawing, aching need. She gasped his name over and over again.

His mouth enclosed hers and while they kissed she felt the incredible sensation of fulfilment as he thrust within her, confident yet gentle, and she knew somewhere at the back of her consciousness that he was holding back, judging her reactions, not rushing her.

The tension inside her built and built; she heard herself whimpering, begging for some new, only partly guessed-at fulfilment that was to come. Then, suddenly, every inhibition left her and she knew what she had to do, as she was taken over by a force of passion she had never imagined. Her body writhed of its own accord beneath his, her hands grasped the taut skin over his hips, pulling him down further into her with a desperate need. There was a prick of pain that she hardly noticed, then Rafe's control snapped and with powerful strokes he took her to the brink of release and then over the edge as they clung together in a long, fierce explosion of pure sensation.

Sara clung to his damp body, trying to hold on to that overwhelming sensation, but gradually the wild pulsing died down and she collapsed limply, aware that she had been sobbing; her cheeks were wet with tears. She brushed them away and let her hand rest across Rafe's chest as he lay on his back beside her, his breathing gradually returning to normal.

Presently she lifted her arm and placed it round his neck as he turned to her and laid his mouth against her temple, where the rich red hair sprang away to cascade over the carpet of brown dried leaves.

'That,' he said shakily, 'has made me whole again. It's been a bad time since I left you, sweetheart. I've ached to have my arms round you.' He twirled a strand of her hair between finger and thumb idly and his mouth was whimsical as he said, 'Have you missed me, Sara? Or have you been too busy enjoying the local sights with Alain?'

Sara's brain was beginning to function again. Careful, it warned. Don't go over the top just because he wanted to make love to you.

She smiled. 'Wouldn't you like to know?'

He gave her shoulder a shake. 'Don't come that Mona Lisa stuff with me, Sara Bennett! Have you missed me?'

'Ye-es, I suppose I have, a little. Mind you, I've quite enjoyed not having you needling me all the time.'

He groaned. 'That's all in the past. I put up a good fight, but I acknowledge defeat.'

His mouth found hers again, lingered luxuriously. His hand began to wander over her silky back. 'From now on it's sweetness and light all the way,' he murmured.

Sara rubbed her cheek against his. 'I'll believe that when I see it,' she chuckled.

This was just fooling; it was a release after that almost unbearable tension, but something was missing, something that she longed for, now more than ever. He'd wanted her, it had been a bad few days for him—that was all. No mention of love.

Now he'd had her, so what next? she wondered with an awful sinking inside. And oh, heavens—he would see Denise and remember—and compare . . . She had forgotten about Denise, she had forgotten everything in the intoxication of seeing Rafe again, of making love. It was terrifying what passion could do to you.

She was suddenly aware that it had gone quite dark. There was a sultry closeness in the small clearing and there seemed no air to breathe. The first low roll of thunder sounded in the distance.

Rafe pulled himself up. 'We'd better get covered, there's going to be a storm.' He dragged on his trousers, reached for Sara's sundress and panties and tossed them over to her. 'Damn bad timing,' he grumbled.

She got to her feet, fumbling into her clothes. Thunderstorms arrived quickly in this part of the world; she remembered the bad ones they had had when she lived in Paris. She had grown almost to enjoy them.

A white flash lit the darkness of the clearing under the trees and the first heavy spots of rain pattered on to the leaves above.

'Come on, we'll make a dash for it.' Rafe grasped Sara's hand and together they pushed their way through the tangle of branches. By the time they reached the hotel the rain was pelting down, bouncing off the marble surround of the deserted swimming pool, standing in puddles on the sun-dried grass of the lawns.

'You run in quickly and dry off,' gasped Rafe, dashing the rain out of his eyes. 'I'll have to get my bag from the car.' He paused long enough to put his hand over her breast, where the cotton dress clung wetly, emphasising the soft swell beneath, and Sara felt an almost painful thrill of pleasure.

She heard his laughing voice close to her ear. 'I could enjoy a repeat performance if it weren't so public here!' He touched her mouth with his, and the brief contact, with the rain running down their faces, was deliciously erotic.

Sara dashed round to the side door and let herself

into the apartment and made straight for the bathroom. In a rainbow dream she took a warm shower and towelled her hair, slipped into a cotton T-shirt dress in palest lemon-yellow, stared into her face as she applied make-up, repeating over and over again to herself the words Rafe had said. 'I came back for you, I couldn't stay away.'

Could she read into those words the meaning she wanted so badly—that he loved her? No, she told herself honestly, she couldn't. But they were lovers, and that would have to be enough—beyond that she wouldn't let herself think.

In the living-room she stood at the window and watched the storm, which by now was quite spectacular. Lightning sheeted across the sulphur-grey sky, thunder rumbled incessantly, rain sluiced down the long window and rushed in a torrent across the paved area into the rockery. The plants would be grateful, Sara thought, and the whimsical idea struck her that she herself had been rather like a parched flower until Rafe came back to her. She had opened to him as the flowers were opening to rain, drinking it in, longing for more.

She had been standing at the window for perhaps a quarter of an hour when she began to feel uneasy. The storm was getting more majestic all the time, the thunder crashing overhead, the lightning continuous. No need to worry, she told herself, Rafe would be here soon. But what if he'd encountered Denise?

She should have told him before this that Denise had turned up at the hotel and had been asking for him. She felt slightly guilty that she hadn't. She wasn't supposed to know that Denise was Rafe's ex-wife, but she *had* known, and Rafe would realise that she had known.

Perhaps he was talking to Denise now—perhaps she was saying, 'But I told that girl who's working for you that I wanted to see you. I told her it was urgent.'

She couldn't let that happen; she had to find Rafe and warn him before he saw Denise. She hurried along the short passage that led to the hotel lounge, which was empty except for the dark, lanky girl behind the reception desk. 'Have you seen Monsieur Jordan?' Sara asked her.

The girl's customary expression was one of faint boredom, but now her face was pink with excitement. 'Monsieur Jordan has gone out with Monsieur Savin to search for the little boy. His mother left him in charge of Madame Brouet, the housekeeper, you understand, but he escaped when she wasn't looking and he hasn't come back.' The girl seemed to be enjoying the drama as she waved her hands towards the front entrance, where Sara saw the plump figure of the housekeeper craning her neck in all directions. '*Madame*, she is quite distracted!'

Sara was icy cold. Flip out in this storm—alone! 'Where have they gone to look for him? Quickly—tell me!'

She must have looked fierce, for the girl quailed visibly. 'The gentlemen thought he could be hiding in the garage block or one of the outhouses—they are searching there.'

'And where's his mother?' Sara snapped.

'Madame Franklin, she is still out. She enquired for a hairdresser.' The girl flinched as an ear-splitting crack of thunder sounded overhead. She pulled a face. 'I am not very brave or I myself would go and search. Where can he be, the poor little one? He will be afraid of the thunder.'

There was no time to waste. Sara ran back to the bedroom, snatched a raincoat from the wardrobe and dashed out through the side door, pulling the belt tightly round her and dragging the hood over her hair as she went. It was almost dark under the trees in the wood, and the branches scratched her bare legs as she pushed through them. Once she lost her way completely and had to stop and get back on to the path, soggy now as the rain bucketed down. She found herself praying aloud, 'Please let him be there!' She kept thinking of the lake and the way a small child might be tempted to paddle there, with memories of seaside holidays, perhaps. She kept remembering the tangling weeds just below the surface.

At last the lake was before her, its steel-grey surface pitted by raindrops as big as pennies, the gazebo a dark shape at the far corner of the shore. When she reached it Sara had barely enough breath left to shout, 'Flip—Flip—are you there?' but another crash of thunder drowned her words.

At first she thought the gazebo was empty. Then she saw something move at the end of the bench and heard a faint sound like a kitten mewing. Oh, thank God, thank God, he was here, he was safe!

The boy was curled up on the floor like a small, frightened animal. As Sara crouched down beside him he lifted his head and said something. His words were lost in the noise of rain and thunder, but he seemed to recognise her when she put her arms round him and lifted him up to stand on the bench. His clothes were quite dry—he must have been here for ages, since before the rain started.

But now she had to get him back to the hotel—and

quickly. She peeled off her raincoat and put her lips close to his ear. 'Hop up, Flip, and I'll give you a piggy-back ride to your mama.'

She turned her back, and he climbed up obediently and clamped his arms tightly round her neck. She drew the raincoat as well as she could round both of them, fastening one of the buttons to anchor it, hung on to his feet and set off at a trot through the trees.

The return journey seemed easier and faster—probably because her fears had been allayed—and finally she came within sight of the welcome lights of the hotel. Best of all, Rafe was coming to meet her.

He didn't wait for explanations, he simply took the little boy from her and carried him into the light and warmth of the hotel foyer where the housekeeper, an ample lady in a shiny black dress, was flapping about like a worried hen.

When she saw Flip safe and sound she began to give thanks to the Almighty and an assortment of saints. 'His mother, she has not returned yet—what will she say when she is told what has occurred? *Le petit*, he ran out of my kitchen when I did not look. One moment he is sitting at the table with his drawing and the next—pouf!—when I turn round he is gone . . .'

Rafe said impatiently, 'Yes—well, you can do the explaining later, *madame*. Just now this child needs a hot bath.' He threw a glance at Sara's wet dress and soaking hair and added, '*Both* these children. Come along, the two of you.'

He picked Flip up in one arm, threw the other round Sara and made straight for the apartment. 'I'll look after the boy—you strip and wrap yourself up in the duvet while you're waiting for the bath.'

Sara did as she was told without demur. Her teeth were chattering, whether from cold and wet or from nerves she didn't know. Rafe had left the bathroom door open and she went in, swathed in the blue duvet, and watched the proceedings. Flip was sitting in a tub of hot water and Rafe was rubbing his back briskly, talking reassuringly all the time. 'That feels good, does it? He'll be OK now, won't you, old fellow? Feeling warmer now, are you?'

Sara watched the two of them, her heart squeezing up inside her. Flip was chuckling happily, enjoying the attention he was getting. She might be doing his mother an injustice, but somehow she couldn't imagine Denise making a fun occasion out of bathtime.

Flip spotted Sara standing in the doorway and his mouth broke into a lovely smile. 'I came to play. You said we could play again.'

'So I did.' Sara came and stood beside the bath. 'And then the thunder came along and the rain—was that it?'

Flip nodded. 'I was a *little* bit afraid, but not very,' he said stoutly. 'I knew you would come.'

'And I did come, so it's OK now, isn't it?' She bit her lip. He must have been sitting there waiting for her all the time she and Rafe had been . . . had been . . .

'That'll do now.' Rafe hauled the slippery little body out of the bath and wrapped Flip in a thick, fleecy towel. 'Let's go and find some dry clothes for you, shall we?' To Sara he added, 'Have a good soak, sweetheart, you look like a little drowned mouse.'

She pulled a face at him. 'Thanks very much. You're a trifle damp yourself.' After their first soaking he had changed into an Aran sweater and tough jeans, and now he brushed the film of rain away as Sara shut the bathroom door on him.

It was lovely to immerse herself in the hot water, but this time round was no time for dreaming. Any moment now Rafe was going to learn who Flip was, and that Denise was staying in the hotel, and she mustn't leave him alone with Flip until she was there to provide some sort of explanation. She wasn't looking forward to it.

When she'd dried herself briskly and got into jeans and a cream wool top she went, a little apprehensively, into the living-room. Flip was sitting on the edge of a sofa solemnly crunching a shortbread biscuit. Rafe came in from the kitchen with a mug of hot milk. 'This seemed a good idea,' he said, holding out the mug to Flip and steadying the child's hands to drink.

Flip evidently approved of hot milk. He took a long gulp of it and looked up into eyes as dark as his own. 'Thank you,' he said politely, and held on to the mug between his two hands.

'Independent, aren't we?' grinned Rafe. 'What's your name, buster?'

Sara caught her breath. 'Look, Rafe, there's something . . .' she began. But Flip had already launched into his announcement. 'My name is Philip John Franklin—but you can call me Flip if you like.' He lifted the mug and drank some more milk quite unconcernedly.

Rafe's face had gone very white. His head jerked round to Sara, his eyes asking a question. She nodded slightly. 'I guessed . . .' she faltered. 'I should have warned you . . .'

'You bloody well should!' He gripped her arm. 'Let's get out of here, I want to talk to you.'

He dragged her into the hall. 'Now,' he said, 'what's all this about?'

'Let go of my arm,' she fumed, 'you're hurting me!' As he removed his hand she backed against the wall, eyeing him apprehensively. The black eyes glared at her. It was almost impossible to remember now, only a short time ago, they had looked into her own eyes with such tenderness.

'Well?' he rasped. 'Denise is here, is she? And that is her boy?'

It was no good trying to evade the issue. 'Yes.'

'And you say you guessed she was my ex-wife? Why?' He shook her shoulders, his face close to hers. '*Why?*'

Sara moistened her dry lips. 'Her name—the colour of her hair—and—and because she tried to find out from me where you were, and if you were coming back. Naturally, I told her that I knew you *weren't* coming back. That's all. What was I supposed to do? It wasn't my business.'

Rafe's face was a hard mask. 'You should have warned me before we . . .'

'Before we made love?' She met his dark angry gaze, green eyes flashing. 'All right, perhaps I should, but you didn't give me much time to think, did you? *And what difference would it have made if I had told you? Would you have gone looking for her instead?*

Suddenly his shoulders sagged. 'Denise, here!' he groaned. 'And she gave that bastard Franklin a son—after what she did to me. God, I could kill them both!'

Sara stared helplessly at the bowed head, knowing there was nothing she could do or say that would help him. She said, 'I must get back to Flip—the child's had a bad fright. He's been very plucky.'

She moved sideways, because Rafe's body was blocking her way forward, but before she could get away he reached out and gripped her shoulders, drawing her towards him. 'Sara, I . . .' She wasn't to know what he would have said, for at that moment the door of the apartment burst open and Denise appeared, closely followed by Alain, looking, for once, rather flustered. He lifted both hands questioningly.

'You have found the little boy? You have him safe? Ah, that is good.'

Ignoring the Frenchman, Denise walked straight across the hall and stood in front of Rafe. Alain must have told her of Rafe's return, for she showed no surprise at seeing him. She raised her wonderful cloudy grey eyes to his. 'Hello, darling, we meet again.' Her voice was low and husky.

Sara heard Rafe's sharp intake of breath and saw the way his eyes rested on the flawless face with a strange, concentrated scrutiny. 'Hello, Denise,' he said quietly.

She placed a hand with pretty hesitation on his arm and he stood quite still, looking down at the long slim fingers with their almond-shaped, burgundy-enamelled nails, and made no effort either to touch her hand or to move his arm away.

Denise flushed slightly and she dropped her hand to her side. 'I hear you've been rescuing my naughty son. I hope he thanked you nicely.'

Rafe seemed to have to drag his eyes away from her face as he said, 'It's Sara he should thank. She's the one who went out in the storm to find him—and risked pneumonia in the process.' To Sara's intense embarrassment he threw an arm round her shoulder.

Denise hardly managed to conceal her annoyance.

But finally she glanced briefly at Sara. 'How brave of you, dear. I do hope you won't suffer any ill-effects.' She managed to make it sound sincere, but her eyes remained cold.

Immediately she turned her gaze back to Rafe. 'It's so wonderful to see you again, Rafe.' She sighed. 'All those years! It's like another life.'

'Yes, isn't it?' He didn't remove his hand from Sara's shoulder. She could feel his strong fingers biting into her flesh through the thin wool of her top.

'We must have a lovely long talk, mustn't we?' The big grey eyes turned towards Alain. 'One must be civilised about these things, don't you agree, Monsieur Savin?'

There was more than a touch of cynicism in Alain's smile. *'Mais certainement, madame.'* He looked towards Rafe and Sara, standing together. 'And where is the little runaway?'

'Flip!' Sara called in the direction of the living-room. 'Your mama is here.'

It must have been obvious to everyone that Flip hadn't run immediately to his mother when she came in, as might have been expected. Now he appeared in the doorway, looking sulky.

Denise pounced on him, holding him carefully away from her beautiful dress. 'Little horror! What have you been up to, giving all these people so much trouble?' She glanced laughingly over her shoulder at Rafe. 'Is this your shirt he's wearing? Isn't it silly—I remember the smell of your aftershave from all those years ago.'

Sara saw Alain's eyebrows rise slightly, and remembered how he'd said, 'He is well rid of her.' But of course he was too well-mannered to show disapproval of Denise's tasteless remark. 'Excuse me, please,' he said. 'Now I must return to my duties. I am so glad the little boy's adventure has not turned out any more disastrous.' He bowed politely and left them, closing the door behind him.

Denise gave a little cry of delight. 'What a sweetie! Frenchmen have such beautiful manners!' She slid a provocative glance at Rafe, who didn't rise to the bait.

There was an awkward little silence. Rafe left Sara's side and went across to hold open the door that Alain had closed. The colour deepened in Denise's cheeks at what could only be construed as a snub. He wasn't going to be won over so easily. But he would go back to her eventually, if she wanted him to—what man wouldn't? Sara thought.

'Rafe, I must talk to you soon,' Denise was saying, serious now. 'Would just before dinner suit you?' She fingered her enormous diamond and emerald ring restlessly. 'My suite is on the first floor—the receptionist will show you.'

Flip had been standing in silence, his eyes moving from one to the other of the grown-ups, frowning puzzledly. Now he ran to Sara. 'Can we play again tomorrow? Please—you promised!' he pleaded in his earnest little voice.

His mother grabbed his hand and pulled him towards her. 'Don't be a little nuisance, Philip. The best place for you is bed.' She turned back to Rafe. 'Shall we say in half an hour—to give me time to get the brat to bed?'

He nodded impassively. 'As you wish.'

Denise lingered a moment longer, studying his face. Then she turned abruptly and led Flip away.

Rafe closed the door behind them. 'Are you all

right?' he said to Sara. 'No ill-effects after two soakings?'

'I'm fine,' she told him brightly.

'You could do with a drink.' He led the way into the living-room. 'And so could I.'

She followed him. There was a curious feeling of unreality about everything now. She tried to think of something to say, but Denise's appearance had put a stop to communication between them.

She guessed that Rafe felt the same way. He brought her a small glass of brandy and water and poured one for himself, his face set and expressionless, and she knew his thoughts were miles away.

She drank the brandy and struggled to suppress the cough that stung her throat. She had a ridiculous feeling that she mustn't draw attention to herself—that she had no place in Rafe's life now. What had happened out there in the wood had been, for him, a passing need—nothing to do with love, or sharing.

Neither of them had sat down. Rafe was standing with his back to the big drawing-board, where Sara's work of the past three days was displayed. He wouldn't want to examine it now. She put down her glass on a side table and said briskly, 'Thanks. I'd better go and get myself tidied up.'

He nodded absently. 'Yes, you do that.'

She got to the door before he said, 'Sara . . .'

She spun round. 'Yes?'

The dark eyes met hers sombrely across the room. 'Oh, never mind—it'll have to wait.' He took his glass over to the drinks cupboard for a refill and Sara escaped to her bedroom.

Here she sank on to the bed and tried to face the situation. There was no doubt in her mind that Denise wanted Rafe back; it had been apparent in her every look, her every gesture. Her plan of campaign was only just beginning, but she would win in the end. She was so unbelievably beautiful. And she could offer Rafe a ready-made family—if he was willing to accept another man's son. His dream of a family life would come true.

Sara lay down and closed her eyes. She felt utterly exhausted in body and mind. So much had happened in the space of such a short time. She had lost her virginity, rescued a child in a thunderstorm, twice got soaked to the skin—and been sliced in two by the sharp, agonising pain of jealousy. She pulled the duvet over her head as if she could shut it all out.

Some time later, through a haze of misery, she heard the front door of the apartment open and close again. Rafe had gone to Denise, obediently, at her bidding, and Sara's heart felt like lead inside her.

CHAPTER EIGHT

THE next thing Sara was aware of was the burring of the bedside phone. She roused herself from a heavy stupor and fumbled for the instrument.

'Sara—just to let you know I shan't be at dinner this evening.' Rafe's voice sounded oddly excited. Sara pictured Denise snuggling up beside him and felt sick. 'Something's come up and I have to go out for a time.' A pause, then, 'It's all been rather a muddle, but we'll sort it out tomorrow. I'm sorry this has happened—forgive me, Sara?'

'Rafe, what . . .?' she began, but he had rung off.

She pulled herself up in the bed, pushing the hair out of her eyes. She felt icy cold and hoped she hadn't caught a chill—it would be too ignominious to meet Rafe tomorrow with bleary eyes. Tomorrow would be a time for hanging on to her pride, for putting on a convincing act as the modern career girl she had once—a long, long time ago—convinced herself she intended to become. A girl who didn't expect commitment from a man on the strength of a little lovemaking. A girl who could laugh and walk away—just as men did.

Rafe would perhaps be feeling a trifle guilty, but he wouldn't blame himself too much. He'd made no promises to her—quite the reverse, in fact. He'd made it clear all along that another marriage was, for him, out of the question. Remarriage to your first wife wouldn't count, of course, she thought bitterly. Had

Denise already secured her divorce from Flip's father, or was she hedging her bets—waiting until she could be sure of getting Rafe back?

Sara didn't doubt that Rafe and Denise were together. Once Flip was in bed they would probably drive to some hotel where they weren't known. Oh God! Sara muttered, gulping helplessly and covering her face with her hands to shut out the picture that conjured itself up in her mind. It couldn't happen . . .! Rafe wouldn't behave like that. She wouldn't believe it. And yet . . .

Stop it, Sara! she screamed inwardly to herself. Have a bit of pride and self-respect. Put on your favourite dress and go in to dinner as if nothing had happened. There won't be any more surprises to cope with today.

It was as if some malignant fate were listening. Just then there was a knock on the front door of the apartment. Sara half fell off the bed and went to open the door.

Denise stood there, groomed to perfection, her glowing hair as smooth as ever, her white silk halter-neck shirt showing a good deal of cleavage but not a single crease. If she had just put an active four-year-old to bed she showed no sign of it.

'May I come in?'

Sara realised that her mouth had fallen open and she was staring at the other woman as if she were a ghost.

She pulled herself together and held the door open. 'Of course.' She led the way into the living-room.

'What a perfectly fascinating apartment!' Denise arranged herself carefully in a deep lounge chair, looking around at the pictures, the ornaments, all the precious collector's items.

What was this—a social visit? 'Can I get you a drink?' Sara offered, hanging on to what little composure she had left.

'Thank you. Whisky, please.'

There was silence while Sara poured drinks for them both. She'd already had brandy, she remembered, but something more was needed. Dutch courage, they called it. Why Dutch? she wondered idiotically, and sat down opposite Denise and waited.

Denise crossed her gorgeous silken legs, settling back in her chair. 'I thought it would be a good time for us to have a little talk, Sara.' She smiled with charming frankness. 'But first I must thank you again for rescuing poor little Philip in that dreadful thunderstorm. I'd gone off to have my hair done in the town and I'd left him in the charge of the housekeeper.' She clicked her tongue. 'These women!'

'Is Flip—Philip—all right?' Sara asked quickly.

'Fast asleep. I gave him half of one of my sleeping tablets—it always works like a charm.'

Sara was appalled. To give a little child drugs as a regular thing—it was a crime!

'He's getting to the difficult age,' Denise sighed. 'He needs discipline, but it's so difficult to find a nanny who will stay with us. You see, my husband travels a great deal and he likes to have me with him, but . . .' she shrugged delicately '. . . to cart a nanny and a small child around is a dreadful chore. Which will explain my difficulty, of course, and the plan I've just been suggesting to Rafe.'

Some of this must make sense, Sara thought, but so far it hadn't. 'Plan?' she echoed.

'Hasn't he told you? I thought he would have done. From what he said I took it that you and he were lovers, so of course my plan would concern you too.'

This had gone on quite long enough. Sara could feel anger rising inside her like a rushing tide. 'I really can't see that any of this concerns me, Mrs Franklin. Please say what you have to say and then, if you'll excuse me . . .' She glanced towards the door.

Denise made a little *moue* of apology and gracefully stretched out a hand. 'Please forgive me, my dear, if I've taken too much for granted. I really came to enlist your help. You see, I've put to Rafe the idea of taking the boy off my hands for good. It seems a sensible thing for everyone.'

Sara felt her eyes widen. This was incredible, she must have got it wrong. 'You mean—you want Rafe to—adopt Flip—Philip?'

Denise smiled tolerantly. 'Oh, no, there's no need for him to *adopt* Philip, the registration papers are all in order.' She sipped her whisky delicately. 'Hasn't the penny dropped yet? In case he hasn't mentioned it, Rafe is Philip's father.'

Sara gasped. 'I don't believe it!'

'Don't you? No, Rafe didn't at first, but I think I've managed to convince him. Anyway, he's gone off to Paris to check up with my husband, and after that . . .' she shrugged ' . . . the decision is with him. And here is where you come in, Sara.'

'Me?' Sara echoed woodenly. This conversation seemed to be happening to someone else.

'Well, isn't it obvious? You're in love with the man—anyone can see that. If you play your cards right, Rafe will marry you, and then Philip will have a mummy as well as a daddy.' The perfect mouth twisted in a mocking little smile. 'Rafe always wanted a nice, cosy family.'

'Don't you love your son at all?' Sara asked. Soon she was going to be furiously, bitterly angry, but just now there was ice inside her veins.

'Oh, sometimes he's quite sweet. I haven't seen very much of him—there's always been a nanny on tap. Up to now, that is. I guess I'm just not the maternal type.'

'And does your husband know that Philip isn't his son?'

The beautiful grey eyes seemed to harden. 'Oh, yes, he knows.'

Subject closed, Sara thought. She wondered briefly what lay behind those four terse words, but it wasn't really important.

'So,' she said very quietly—and now a hot tide of anger was beginning to rise inside her, melting the ice, 'you came to ask me to use any influence I have with Rafe to persuade him to fall in with your plan?'

Denise laughed easily. 'Well done! You're a clever girl, I knew you'd see the point in the end.'

Sara got to her feet. There was a trembling in her limbs which she controlled by an effort. 'You're right, Mrs Franklin, I do see the point, and I don't like what I see. I think your suggestions and innuendoes are insulting, and I'd be pleased if you'd leave now.'

Denise rose languidly. 'Oh, dear, and I thought I was doing you a good turn!'

Sara examined the perfect face. The grey eyes were cold now, the beautiful mouth peevish. 'I doubt if you've ever done anyone a good turn in your life, Mrs Franklin—except yourself, that is.' She walked across the room and opened the front door. Somehow she must hold on to her precarious dignity for a few moments longer.

Denise rose and lounged gracefully to the door. 'Don't be a silly girl,' she smiled with a not-very-successful effort at hauteur. 'In spite of what Rafe may have told you, I think he'll be ready to marry you now, and you'll be a fool if you turn him down, my dear.'

Sara's rage came to boiling point. 'Get out,' she gritted. 'Get out and stay out!' She saw Denise's amazed expression of outrage before she slammed the door on her.

At half-past nine the phone buzzed, and Sara pulled herself stiffly out of the deep chair where she had been curled up like a hurt animal for what seemed like a lifetime. 'Sara?' It was Alain's voice. 'I did not see you at dinner. I am told that Rafe is not in the hotel at present, and I ask myself if you are all right after your soaking. You are not ill?'

'No, I'm fine, thanks, Alain.' She made her voice normal. 'I didn't feel like dinner—just a bit of a headache.'

'*Tiens*, tiens, that won't do at all. I will ask them to prepare a tray for you. No, don't say anything, Sara—I insist.'

She sighed as she replaced the receiver. Alain was a dear, but she didn't really want food. She didn't want anything except answers to a great many questions.

She heard again Rafe's voice, so softly loving against her lips. 'I came back for you, Sara, I couldn't stay away.' That was what he had said. Could she believe it, or had he come back because Denise had phoned him in London and told him she was here and wanted to see him? Had he come running back at Denise's bidding?

He had appeared to be genuinely surprised to find that Denise was here and that Flip was her son. But probably he was an adequate actor. Had he seen Denise before he came looking for Sara in the gazebo beside the lake? And had she told him then that Flip was his son? Had his lovemaking in the wood been a softening-up process so that she, Sara, would readily consent to anything he suggested?

'If you play your cards right, Rafe will marry you,' that horrible woman had said. *Would he*? *Would he indeed?* And she was expected to be flattered and grateful, was she? Sara seethed with impotent humiliation. She began to see the whole thing as an elaborate plot between Denise and Rafe, in which she, Sara, would play her part as a sort of super-nanny who would be there to fall into bed with him any time he required her.

She pressed her hands to her throbbing temples. What was the truth? She'd been wrong once, perhaps she was wrong again. But it would have been almost less painful, she thought now, if he *had* been going to remarry Denise, if he had still been in love with her. At least that would have been an honest emotion.

There was a tap on the door and Alain appeared, bearing a tray. 'I came to satisfy myself that you had not suffered too bad effects of your soaking,' he said, placing the tray on a low table beside Sara's chair.

He looked round the big living-room. 'It is not warm enough here.' He went across to the powerful electric fire and switched it on. 'And is your headache any better, Sara? I have brought you some tablets, in case you have not got any with you.'

Sara's eyes misted. 'You really are kind, Alain.'

He grinned and spread out his hands. 'Somebody should look after you, and my friend Rafe has rushed off to Paris, I am told.' There was a touch of censure in his voice.

'It was—very important.'

'Oh, yes? Well, perhaps. Now you must eat some dinner and I will sit here and watch you and share some coffee with you.' He settled comfortably in a deep chair opposite.

The roast duck with an onion and tomato sauce was no doubt delicious, but Sara might just as well have been eating baked beans or fish fingers. She struggled through a little of the peach tart and drank two cups of black coffee.

'That is better,' said Alain, removing the tray. He sat down again and crossed his legs. 'Now, tell me why you are unhappy, *ma chère*.'

'I'm not . . .' Sara began, and two large tears gathered and trickled down her cheeks.

'No?' Alain smiled gently. 'It is Rafe, is it not? You are in love with him?'

She examined her fingers, lacing themselves on her lap. 'I suppose I am,' she admitted miserably. 'Silly, isn't it?'

'Love is never silly,' Alain said firmly. 'You have quarrelled—yes?'

She dabbed at the tears with her fingers. 'No, nothing like that. It's just . . .' She hesitated. The temptation to confide in this sympathetic Frenchman, who knew about love, was strong, but an odd sense of pride made her resist it. '—Just that it's all so hopeless.'

'Nothing is ever hopeless, little Sara—except death,' he added sadly, and she knew he was thinking of Marguerite. 'Now you must take these tablets for your headache and they will help you to sleep. And tomorrow, everything will look very much better.'

He got to his feet and picked up the tray. 'Goodnight, little one.' He touched her bright hair. 'Sleep well.'

Perhaps it was exhaustion, or the tablets, or the relief at admitting aloud that she was in love with Rafe—whatever the reason, Sara fell into a heavy sleep as soon as her head touched the pillow. But Alain had been wrong—in the morning *nothing* looked better, in spite of the warm sunshine that had followed the storm of yesterday.

But life—and work—must go on. Alain, for all his sympathetic understanding, wanted his gallery built and she was here to help build it. The waiter brought breakfast as usual, and she ate croissants and apricot preserve and took her last cup of coffee to the drawing-board. She would have to work hard today to make up for the time lost yesterday.

She had been working for more than an hour when she heard the door of the apartment open. It could only be Rafe, and her stomach went hollow. She kept her eyes fixed on the large plan sheet in front of her, putting off the moment when she would have to look round and meet his eyes.

The thick carpet muffled his footsteps, and the next thing she knew was that his arms had come round her from behind and he was hugging her tightly, his cheek buried in her hair, and her treacherous body was melting at the feel of him, at the smell of his body, warm and intimate.

He pulled her to her feet, turning her round, and the need to throw her arms round his neck was a physical pain that had at all costs to be resisted. She had to keep her cool now, wait until she saw which way he meant to play the next act in the drama.

'Let me look at you.' He was smiling broadly; he looked like a man whose dearest wish has been granted. Which, thought Sara, it probably had. He had acquired a son.

She put a teasing note in her voice as she said, 'Well, have you brought back a cricket bat for Flip?'

Rafe took the point immediately. 'Cricket bats are in short supply in Paris,' he grinned. 'But I managed to get a super model Renault.' He fished in his pocket for the tiny model car and put it on the front flange of the drawing-table. 'Do you think he'll like it—it won't be too old for him?'

'Oh, I'm sure he'll love it,' Sara said.

He drew her over to a sofa and sat her down beside him. 'So—you know?'

She nodded. 'Your ex-wife came here last evening, specially to explain everything to me.' He could make what he liked of that.

'Damn!' he burst out. 'I wanted to tell you myself.' He laid his head against the high back of the sofa. 'Honestly, Sara, I feel as if I'd been poleaxed. It was so totally unexpected. Even now I can't quite come to terms with the fact that I have a son. When Denise told me I laughed at her. It was a while before I took it seriously at all, but when she came up with dates and—certain facts, I began to believe it might be true. A visit to Philip Franklin in Paris put the matter beyond doubt as far as I'm concerned.'

He sighed deeply. 'Flip's such a grand kid, I liked him straight away. He's full of guts, isn't he? The way he took that frightening experience last night—he must have been scared stiff, out in that storm, but he didn't even cry.' His dark eyes were shining; he shook his head wonderingly.

Suddenly he seemed to remember that Sara was there. 'How did you know where to look for him, by the way?'

A shadow seemed to have fallen across the sunny room. Just ahead loomed something dark and painful. But *I* mustn't cry either, she told herself. 'He wandered out to the site one day when you were away,' she said, keeping her voice carefully under control. 'He seemed lonely and I played with him for a little while. I guessed he might have found his way back there and been caught in the storm.'

Rafe nodded, pleased. 'You—like him?'

'Of course I do—very much. He's a dear little boy.'

His arm closed round her. 'Then you won't mind too much if we start off our married life with a ready-made family, Sara, darling?'

Here it was, then, what she had dreaded, and now it had actually happened she was quite, quite calm.

'Our . . . did you say our . . . married life?'

'That's right,' said Rafe with hateful smugness. He leaned over and kissed the tip of her nose.

'I don't seem to remember your asking me to marry you.'

'Oh, surely—I must have done. Should I have gone down on one knee as of yore?' Composing his expression, he actually did kneel down on the shaggy white carpet. 'Miss Sara Bennett, will you do me the honour of accepting my hand in marriage?'

Her eyes were on a level with his. 'Thank you, but no,' she said, and thought with sudden panic, What am I doing? Throwing away a chance of paradise. But *would* it be paradise—marriage to a man who needed you as a kind of final piece to complete his jigsaw-puzzle picture of the perfect family?

There was a trace of uneasiness in his laugh as he got up and slid down beside her. 'No need to carry the charade too far, darling. It isn't necessary to say "no" modestly to the first few proposals in these enlightened days.'

'I'm serious,' she said, and she saw from the sudden hardening of his mouth that he was beginning to believe her.

'I won't accept this. Out there in the woods together—it was perfect. I thought it was for you too.'

Sara nodded. 'Of course it was. A perfect initiation. I suppose it had to happen some time,' she added, trying to make it sound casual. 'But I didn't think of marriage.' Liar—of course you did, what girl wouldn't? 'You see, Rafe, I haven't forgotten all the things you said to me about marriage. A man-trap, you called it. Well, I didn't set any trap.'

'But . . .' he began angrily, but she held up a hand to stop him.

'I certainly wouldn't marry you because we'd slept together once,' she went on calmly. 'Or because you happen to need me to complete your "happy family"—to be a cosy wife, mother to Flip. Your "Little Grey Home in the West", you called it, didn't you?' Now that she had started, the words were pouring out of their own accord. 'Besides,' she went on, 'what I told you was as true as what you told me. I don't want marriage—not yet. I've got plans for my future.'

Rafe's face had turned very white. She could have made him happy and instead she had shattered his dream once again. Anguish, and a kind of guilt, gnawed at her, and she almost relented and put her arms round him and told him she hadn't meant any of it.

But instead she said very quietly, 'I won't be—*used*, Rafe.'

He stared at her as if he were seeing her for the first time. 'I see. Then there's nothing more to be said.' He got up and stood frowning down at her. 'Do I take it that you still wish to continue with this project here?' he said icily.

'That's for you to decide,' she said. 'But I think it would be better, perhaps, if I returned to London, if that's agreeable to you.'

Suddenly his control snapped. 'No, it's not agreeable to me! Nothing's bloody agreeable to me!' His eyes burned like smouldering fires into hers.

'You'll be staying on here?' she asked. What was he going to arrange about Flip? Would the little boy be unhappy at being left in the charge of a strange man? Again her conscience smote her unreasonably. 'I just wondered—about little Flip . . .' she faltered.

'Oh, for God's sake don't put on the pathos!' snarled Rafe. 'It doesn't impress me in the least. I'm responsible now for my son.' He drew in a short breath. 'All right, you can go. I'll arrange it—the sooner the better.'

Sara clenched her hands. 'By the way, I'd better make it clear that I've no intention of resigning from

Jordan's because of—personal matters—unless you throw me out.'

He gave her a sour glance and looked away again quickly. 'You know damn well Dad wouldn't stand for that. You're his favourite girl at present.' All the old bitter irony was back in his voice. Sara winced. Had she done this to him? she thought. Oh, Rafe, why couldn't you have told me you love me? Even if it weren't true I'd have believed you.

Suddenly he turned on her in fury. 'Oh, to hell with the whole bloody thing!' he shouted, and strode out of the room, slamming the door behind him.

Sara was unable to move, her limbs felt sluggish and numb. She kept seeing the glow of happy excitement in his face when he first came into the room, all ready to tie up the loose ends of his new life-plan. And she had spoilt it all for him.

But what about *my* life-plan? she thought. Her plan to work her way up in her profession? He hadn't mentioned that, he'd just taken for granted that she would agree to everything he wanted—that she would give it all up to be a wife and mother. If he'd loved me I would have done, she thought. I'd have done anything for him, given up anything. But her career was all she had now—probably all she would ever have, for it didn't seem remotely possible that she would feel for any other man what she felt for Rafe.

Presently she got up stiffly, like an old woman, and walked to her drawing-board. She must finish the job she had begun. These were the all-important working drawings, and when they were completed the first part of her involvement with the project would be finished. Someone else could take over from here.

She looked down at her careful, intricate plans and elevations and saw, instead, the little model car that Rafe had put on the ledge of the drawing-board. She had to stand quite still for minutes, fighting back tears, her fingernails digging into her palms. Then she lifted the toy and placed it carefully on a side table where Rafe would find it. After that she went back to complete her work.

Some time in the early evening—Sara had lost count of time—Rafe returned. He looked towards the table where Sara's lunch rested untasted on its tray. 'You haven't eaten your lunch,' he said abruptly.

She glanced carelessly over her shoulder at the table. 'I forgot about it.' In case he should think that she'd been sitting here weeping, she added, indicating her drawing-board, 'I wanted to get all this tidied up before I leave.'

He nodded as if he weren't very interested. 'I've booked a flight for you—tomorrow afternoon. Alain happens to be driving into Paris and he's offered to give you a lift to the airport. He'll be leaving about ten.'

'That's very kind of him,' Sara said woodenly.

He seemed on the verge of making some sarcastic retort and then he stopped. He strode across to the window and stood staring out, frowning, hands stuck deep into trouser pockets. 'I've been thinking over what you said, Sara, and I've come reluctantly to the conclusion that maybe you're right—certainly you're justified. I've behaved like a real bastard to you.'

Rafe, apologising! She couldn't believe it.

When she said nothing he turned and came back to her. 'All I can say is that I'll do my best to further your career with Jordan's. I'm sure you're going to be a great asset to our firm,' he finished stiffly.

'Thank you,' she said. She should be appreciating this new, reasonable Rafe. Instead she almost wished he would revert to his old, maddening ways. At least they seemed honest. She didn't know the man standing before her at all.

'Shall we meet at dinner?' he said formally, but she shook her head.

'I have several things to finalise . . .' she indicated her work '. . . and I don't want to take time off to shower and change. Perhaps you'd ask them to bring something in for me here.'

Rafe nodded. 'Just as you wish. I'll deliver your message.'

'Thank you,' she said again, but he'd already gone out of the room.

Sara lay awake dry-eyed most of the night, wondering how she was going to take her leave of Rafe next morning and if she would see Flip again. She had this odd feeling of having let Flip down, although common sense told her that it was illogical. Flip was Rafe's responsibility, as he had informed her with such crushing emphasis. As for the prospect of leaving Rafe—she couldn't bear, yet, to think about it. Love was the worst wound of all, it didn't heal. She was going to have to carry around the despairing black weight inside her, and somehow she would have to learn to live with it.

She fell into a heavy sleep just before dawn, and when she wakened it was after nine o'clock. Alain wanted to start out at ten—she'd have to hurry. She showered and dressed, trying to concentrate on what she was doing because if she let her mind wander she was going to howl like a dog who had lost his master. She packed her bag and couldn't stop remembering the last time she had gone through this routine—the high hopes she had started out with. The euphoria of being selected from the other juniors to come here and work on the plans for the gallery, the confidence she'd felt that she could cope with Rafe's antagonism—even make him value her and like her a little.

Like her! Suddenly a great shudder made her drop the jumper she was packing and sink down on to the bed, remembering the feel of his arms around her, his hands on her body, his mouth on hers. All gone, all finished! A great sob rose in her throat.

I can't do it, she thought frantically, jumping to her feet. I can't give all that up. I must go to him, try to explain, tell him I'll do anything he wants . . .

The phone buzzed beside the bed. 'Am I too early for you, Sara?' Alain's pleasant voice enquired. 'There is no great hurry, but we ought to set out in half an hour or so. Rafe has already left, with the little boy. He is driving Madame Franklin to Paris, I understand, to join her husband. Make a good breakfast and we shall meet in the foyer when you are ready, *oui*?'

Too late, too late!

'Yes,' said Sara, and remembered to add, 'Thank you, Alain.'

Sara didn't remember much about the drive to Paris. Alain, bless him, must have known something of what had happened, and he drove quickly and almost silently, merely putting in a remark or two about some interesting part of the countryside they were passing through, not expecting any response.

At the airport, when he had parked he car, he took charge of everything for her, gave her her ticket and checked on her flight. 'We have a little time to spare. You could drink a coffee, Sara?'

In the coffee-shop, sitting together, it was impossible any longer to keep up the pretence that this was an ordinary, happy departure. 'I am sad for you, Sara,' Alain said simply, his kind brown eyes searching her white face and dark-circled eyes. 'It has not worked out, has it?'

Sara shook her head, unable to speak. She stared out at the throng in the concourse outside and the figures were a blur of moving colour.

'I cannot promise you that grief will pass,' Alain went on gently. 'Only that it becomes a little more bearable. And—what is your English saying?—while there is life there is hope.' He waited for a moment, then added, 'I will continue to believe that one day you will come back and see your beautiful gallery when it is built, and that you will be very happy. You will come, yes?'

She swallowed hard. 'That would be wonderful, Alain.' It would be more than wonderful, she thought, with a terrible empty grief, it would be a miracle.

Alain stayed by her side until the last possible moment, and when the time came that he could accompany her no further he put a hand on her shoulder and kissed her on both cheeks.

'*Au revoir*, little Sara,' he said, smiling, 'Not *adieu*.'

She remembered his words as the plane lifted into the air and she looked down at the Paris she had left so many times before. She had always been sad to leave, but this time it wasn't merely sadness, it was heartbreak.

'Not *adieu*,' Alain had said.
But it *was* goodbye. Goodbye, Rafe, goodbye, love.
When they met again it would be as strangers.

CHAPTER NINE

'IT's good to have you back with us, Sara. I hope you're not too sad to be leaving France with September nearly here. September's always my favourite month.'

Sara stood beside the senior partner's desk, where she had gone to report first thing on Monday morning, and tried desperately to think of something to say. Donald Jordan might be surprised if she gave him an honest reply.

She looked down at the polished top of his desk and said, 'I've enjoyed working there very much. It's a beautiful spot.' That at least was part of the truth—the unimportant part.

'Yes, so I believe. I must really take a trip over there myself when they get going on the building work. Rafe was on the phone yesterday and he tells me things are getting lined up very satisfactorily.'

And what else did he tell you? That he'd asked me to marry him and I'd refused? Sara almost laughed aloud. From this distance it seemed unbelievable.

'He was very pleased with the work you did there, Sara. You really distinguished yourself, I gather. You got on well with my son, did you? I know you were a trifle apprehensive at first about working with him.'

She managed a smile somehow. 'Oh, yes, we hit it off splendidly when we started to work together.'

'Good, good. I thought you would.' The senior partner looked up searchingly under the thick dark lashes that were so like his son's. 'Rafe's been having a bad patch lately, but he's come through it now and it looks as if better times were ahead for him. You know, of course, about his discovery that he's the father of a son?'

'Oh yes, he was over the moon about it. Making all sorts of plans.' *Plans that included me, only that's something I mustn't even think about.* Her throat had gone tight; she hoped the senior partner wouldn't prolong this interview. She swallowed hard and said, 'Philip is a dear little boy; I'm sure you'll love him.'

'Indeed I shall. I'm very excited about the prospect of having a grandson. We must all try to make his life a happy one. If only Rafe's mother were still alive, what a difference that would have made.' He sighed deeply. 'But I expect things will work themselves out when he brings the boy back to England with him in a few weeks.'

'I'm sure they will,' Sara murmured.

'Rafe told me particularly to keep you posted about all that goes on at the building site. He was sure you'd be interested—although it seems that you'd come to the end of your involvement there.'

The end. The bitter, bitter end. 'Yes, there really wasn't any need for me to stay on,' Sara said, and wished her voice didn't sound so shrill in the quiet office.

The senior partner nodded, looking at her thoughtfully. He couldn't have guessed, could he? She hadn't given herself away?

'Well, you'll want to get back into harness here now. Bob will put you in the picture; he's been standing in for Rafe. We have several new proposals in the pipeline which I'm sure will interest you.'

He nodded kindly, and Sara escaped to her old station in the design office, her cheeks burning.

She had come in early this morning, knowing that the senior partner always arrived before everyone else, and only now the rest of the staff were drifting in, chatting about their weekends. Bob Stafford came over to her immediately.

'Great to have you among us again, Sara. I want to hear all about the goings-on in France. How about a spot of lunch?' He didn't wait for her to accept; he went on, 'You'll be ready to do some real work now after all that lounging around in posh hotels, eh?'

Sara laughed. It was odd that she found it easier to laugh aloud than to smile. 'Lounging about! You're joking, of course.'

'We'll argue about that over lunch. You'll come?' Bob was much more assured than Sara had known him before. Being in charge of the design office had evidently boosted his confidence.

Sara would much rather have skipped lunch and walked down to the river, but she couldn't allow herself the self-indulgence of gazing into the dark water and thinking dark thoughts. She was back in the real world now; she had left behind in France the emotional world of blissful happiness and agonising pain.

'Thanks, Bob, I'd like that,' she said.

And so she began to get back into harness, as Donald Jordan had called it. The work seemed almost dull after the thrill of working on her own design for the gallery, but she told herself that this was her job and she'd better get on with it. The gallery design was a one-off for her, and wasn't likely to happen again for a long time, if ever.

The worst part of the weeks that followed was that Donald Jordan made a habit of 'keeping her in the picture', as he put it, about what was going on in France. Rafe evidently phoned back to London frequently and his father seemed to take it for granted that Sara would want to know all the details of what was happening there—including snippets of news about Flip.

'The boy seems happy enough to be with Rafe,' Donald Jordan told Sara, stopping at her station on one of his daily tours of inspection round the design office. 'He's found a nice French girl—Annette, the daughter of the new chef at the hotel—to take over the mothering jobs for a time, and they're laying on little trips for the lad. I rather gather that Flip hasn't had very much attention from his mother, and it must be quite a pleasant change for him.'

'Yes, indeed.' Sara smiled brilliantly. Dark thoughts about the 'nice French girl' were skittering ominously around in her mind. *She* could have still been there herself—mothering Flip, going on 'little trips' with Rafe and his son, being part of a family. Had she been quite, quite mad to refuse? Was one-sided love ever enough? She lay awake at night tormenting herself with questions, even though it was too late now to change her mind.

She made herself accept one of Bob's invitations to go to a film with him, but the evening wasn't a success and they both knew it. He didn't ask her again, and she sat in her tiny third-floor flat in the evenings facing a future that stretched out empty and grey ahead of her. She couldn't sleep, she couldn't face preparing proper meals. She lost pounds in weight and there were dark circles under green eyes that no longer shone brilliantly. Even her hair suffered, its rich redness dull and lifeless.

'You're a mess,' she told herself despairingly one Friday evening, sitting in front of her mirror, an empty weekend looming ahead. 'You've got to do something about yourself.'

A new dress. A hair-do. That would be a start.

Saturday morning saw her in Oxford Street, in one of the big department stores. Luck was with her; she managed to get a cancellation and within a few minutes of entering the store's enormous hairdressing salon she was lying back enjoying the luxury of allowing someone else to shampoo her hair.

'A beautiful colour, madam,' remarked the pretty girl in the smart navy and white smock, combing back Sara's wet hair, preparatory to shaping it.

'You think so?' Sara gazed unenthusiastically at the sleek red mane that had caused all the trouble from the very beginning. It looked shades darker, of course, when it was wet—almost another colour.

Another colour! That touched a chord of memory. 'Don't you dare have your hair dyed,' Rafe had said, with his usual arrogance.

The idea hit her like a blow between the eyes. Why not? she thought. It would be a gesture for when he saw her again—a defiant reminder that she was her own person. A little *frisson* of excitement passed through her as she said, 'I suppose there wouldn't be time to change the colour now, would there?'

'Certainly, madam, if you wish. The cancelled appointment was for a semi-permanent colour, so I have time to spare. Shall I bring you the shade card?'

* * *

A different person—Sara felt a different person. She kept catching sight of herself in the long mirrors as she wandered between the dress-stands in the fashion department. She couldn't believe that a couple of hours and a lot of expert attention could make it difficult to recognise herself. Who was this tall young woman with the shining mahogany-brown hair curving softly into her neck? Not the stupid girl who had fallen in love with a man who spurned love and marriage, who had called her a 'man-trap' and then, when it suited his purpose and then only, had proposed to her.

No, Sara was her own girl now, she thought almost happily. A young professional woman on her way up.

A new outfit was indicated. Not a party dress—something simple she could wear in the office. She finally settled for a fine wool suit in darkest bronze, classic in cut, with a slinky skirt, a check orange and brown blouse and a short swingy jacket. Gold earrings, a change of make-up, a pair of bronze pumps. Her bank balance would suffer, but it was worth it, she decided, fighting her way on to the bus with her goodies. She was armed against Rafe Jordan when he finally returned to London.

The following Monday morning he walked unexpectedly into the design office. Sara felt his presence as soon as he came into the room without even raising her head, and her heart gave a great lurch and then throbbed heavily. She couldn't bring herself to look up as he walked towards the door beside her desk which led into his father's office.

He was coming nearer, he would have to pass her own station in a couple of seconds. He was tossing a few words to the occupants of the office in general as he passed down the long room between the rows of drawing-boards, and there were murmured replies.

He had paused now, she could almost feel him looking in her direction. She leant her cheek on her hand, half covering her face as he strode past her into his father's office. She heard his angry voice. 'Dad—where's Sara? Who's that new wench sitting in her place?'

Donald's reply was amused, 'Take another look, son. Girls like a change these days.'

Then Rafe was standing over her. She glanced up in feigned surprise. She'd imagined it for weeks, what it would be like when he came back. She'd practised her voice, her smile, pictured how they would meet, persuaded herself that she wouldn't feel anything very much—just a vague regret.

And now her throat was dry as sand, her heart was thumping, all her inside workings were shaking like jelly.

'What the hell have you done to your hair?' he growled.

'Oh, I got tired of being a redhead.' Somehow she managed a more or less coquettish smile, but the corners of her mouth quivered when she met the dark eyes that stared accusingly down at hers. 'D-don't you like it?' she quavered.

'No, I bloody well don't!' he rasped. He didn't seem to notice that all the other occupants of the room had ceased work and were sitting silent, like an audience anticipating a good, satisfying shoot-out at the crisis of a movie.

Rafe gripped Sara's wrist and lugged her out of her seat. 'Come on, I want to talk to you.'

She stared desperately at her drawing-board. 'I can't—I'm very busy. I . . .'

He wasn't taking the slightest notice and there was nothing she could do about it, except put up a fight, and that was unthinkable. She let him take her through the nearest open door, which was the one into the senior partner's office. She heard the buzz of talk that broke out in the room they had just left, before Rafe kicked the door shut with his heel.

Donald Jordan looked up from his desk, unflappable as ever. Rafe's dark face had a hunted look as he said, 'I want to talk to Sara, Dad—somewhere out of here. I didn't bring my car into town—is it OK if I borrow yours for an hour or two?'

'Help yourself, Rafe, I can take a cab if necessary. In fact, I'm dining out tonight—going straight to the restaurant, so I shan't need the car. I can have that extra drink or two.' There was a definite twinkle in the dark eyes that were so like his son's.

With a muttered word of thanks Rafe hustled Sara out of the door that led through the secretary's office, which was providentially empty, and out into the corridor.

Sara found her voice. 'Look, this is ridiculous, you can't—can't just yank me about like this!'

'Can't I?' Rafe pulled open the lift gate with one hand and pushed her inside with the other.

'I've left my handbag in the office,' she wailed.

'Bad luck!' His jaw was set grimly. 'We'll have to hope that the staff are honest.'

Sara gave it up and allowed him to lead her to the underground car park and thrust her into the senior partner's black Rover.

The way Rafe drove through London reminded her

of the way he had driven out of Paris that day she had arrived there. Could it have been only a few weeks ago? It felt like years.

The penthouse flat in the luxury block was very masculine—charcoal leather furniture and smoked glass tables and huge modern pictures on the walls.

'Dad's flat,' said Rafe, peeling off his jacket and throwing it across a chair. 'When my mother died he sold the house and found himself something as impersonal as possible. He misses her badly still, after six years. Now, then, what'll you drink? OK, don't tell me, you look as if this is what you need.'

He brought her a small whisky and water and stood staring down at her, sunk into the corner of the enormous couch. 'God, I can't get over it. You look terrible! How long will it take to grow back again?'

Sara took a gulp of whisky. 'I think I'll keep it this colour, I rather like it.'

He poured himself a drink and came and sat down in the opposite corner of the couch. 'We'll argue about that later,' he said.

After that he seemed to have nothing left to say, he just sat looking at her in a bemused kind of way.

Sara swallowed, choking on a huge lump in her throat. 'Why did you bring me here? What do you want?'

Rafe went on staring and his eyes were like black pools. She felt she was swimming in them helplessly.

He said, 'I love you, Sara, and you've got to marry me. What do I have to do to make you love me?'

Her eyes flew open in incredulity, she gave a great sob, and then she was in his arms and he was kissing her, murmuring incoherent words of love, kissing her cheeks and her throat and her eyelids and finally her lips, like a man dying of thirst who finds cool, clear water.

After a while he pulled a couple of inches away. 'You will marry me, won't you?'

'Oh, yes—yes, as soon as you like,' she gulped. 'Why didn't you tell me before?'

'I did, and you said you wouldn't. You said . . .'

'I know what I said, it was what you didn't say. You didn't say you l-loved me,' she spluttered. 'And I thought it was just . . .' She stopped. 'You *did* say you loved me, didn't you?'

'Oh, darling!' he groaned. 'I don't know what love is, after all these years, but I know I can't go on without you, I want you with me every minute of the day and night, to look at, to talk to, to laugh with, to work with, to go to bed with. When you're not there the sun seems to go in.'

Sara nodded. 'Me too,' she whispered. 'It's been awful, I've just ached and ached for you.' She buried her face against the warmth of his chest through his thin shirt.

He began to tremble against her. 'Dad won't mind us making ourselves at home.' He got up and pulled her to her feet. He fastened his arm round her and led her out of the room, along a passage, into a big bedroom. He pulled back the burgundy-red cover on the bed. 'This is my room when I stay in town. I think it's been waiting for you for a long time.' He began to undress her slowly, deftly, while ripples of excitement ran through her.

But when her blouse was lying beside the slim bronze-coloured skirt on the floor she turned away from him. His arm came round her, urging her back to face him. 'What's the matter, love? It was wonderful last time.'

She found she was crying. 'It's just—just—I keep remembering Denise, she's so beautiful—and ...'

He covered her lips with his fingers. 'Shush, darling. This is us—now—and I love you, is that enough? It's not much I'm offering you—I'm too old for you and I'm cynical and moody and a rotten bargain ...'

'Oh, you're not, you're not,' she wailed. 'You're wonderful and brilliant and I dissolve into a jelly when you come near me. It's just that—somehow I can't believe you love me. You didn't tell me when you—when you asked me to marry you—before ...'

Rafe shook his head. 'That was a terrible mistake, but I thought you must know. Somehow the words "I love you" seemed too easy to say—sort of shop-soiled.'

'I needed to hear them,' she whispered.

'I know now. I'll keep on telling you over and over again—all the years ahead of us. I love you. I love you. I love you.'

With each repetition a lacy garment dropped beside the others until they lay in a heap. Then his own clothes followed and he was beside her on the big bed, his hands and mouth exploring her body. Gradually a melting softness invaded her limbs; she felt all woman against his male strength as her fingers buried themselves in the springing thickness of his hair and stroked the warm hollow of his neck.

She felt him shudder, and then his hands came up to grasp hers and guide them downwards over his body, and she gloried in the pleasure she was giving him as she stroked and fondled his taut, silky skin, tugging gently at the fuzz of hair that covered his chest. When at last her fingers reached the most crucial place of all and he cried out with explosive force, she felt a tide of triumph sweep over her. *She* could give him this pleasure, she could make him forget everything and everyone that went before.

'Rafe, my love,' she murmured, and pressed herself against him as he covered her with his body, his mouth claiming hers in a deep, thrusting kiss.

She knew he had been holding back, savouring the feel of her hands on him, but now he could hold back no longer. She closed her eyes and sank into a swelling, rising wave of ecstasy as they moved together in a plunging rhythm of loving that went on and on until finally the wave broke and thundered in a wild frenzy and then, slowly, died away and left them both gasping and replete.

When Rafe got his breath back he drew her head on to his shoulder, moulding her body against his. 'Why did I leave it so long? We've wasted days and days. Why didn't I come back before and chance my luck?' he groaned.

'Why didn't you?' Sara snuggled closer.

'Because I'd been such a bloody idiot,' he burst out violently. 'I thought I'd spoilt everything, lost you for good. It never occurred to me that you'd think I just wanted you because I'd got myself a son and I needed a woman to look after him. That's what you did think, wasn't it?'

'Yes,' she nodded, 'I'm afraid I did. I didn't want to be taken for granted—my sticky pride, I suppose. You were so sure you didn't want another marriage, then suddenly when Flip came along, you changed your mind. What was I to think?'

He sighed heavily. 'I know, don't rub it in.'

She said, 'What made you come back and—and

abduct me like that?' She giggled. 'I haven't got over the shock yet!'

He thought for a while. 'I suppose it was Alain who finally showed me what a fool I was. He knew damn well I was pining for you, I must have been a terrible drag around the place after you left. Flip was suffering too—that boy's bright, he knew there was something wrong. He said to me, "Where's Sara gone? Will she come back?" Alain was there at the time and he managed to hold me together when I nearly fell apart. Afterwards, when we were alone after dinner, he said suddenly. "Did you remember to tell that girl you love her"? If not, why don't you go and find her and tell her so?'

'I said you didn't want me—you wanted a career—and he laughed and called me several very unflattering names in French. Next day—yesterday—I put Flip and Annette—this girl I've engaged to look after him—in the car and drove back to London like a crazy thing.' His grip on her tightened. 'When I walked into that office and saw a stranger with dark hair sitting at your desk I thought you'd gone—left for good. My world collapsed and fell apart at that moment. Oh, darling!' His voice shook and he pressed his cheek against the top of her head. 'I really have got you now, haven't I? You won't ever leave me?'

'Just try to make me!'

'And of *course* I don't want you to give up your career; we need you in the firm, you're much too talented to lose. You won't be stuck in front of a drawing-board all day, but you won't be stuck in front of a kitchen sink either. We'll work something out. And when Dad retires in a few years from now and our family is growing up, we'll make you a partner in the firm,' Rafe began to plan happily. He checked himself and added, 'You would like *our* child, wouldn't you?' he asked a little anxiously. 'And you don't mind taking Flip on?'

'Yes,' she said, 'I would. And no, I don't. Any more questions?' she teased.

'Just at the moment I can only think of one. Do I have to spell it out? Dad won't be back for hours, and Flip's well looked after at my home in Hendon.'

'How is he?' she asked, and added, 'My turn to ask questions now.'

'Oh, he's fine—fine. Last time I saw him he was drawing a house—he's going to be an architect.' She heard the love and pride in his voice. Oh, I want to give him a son too, she thought.

'Was he—was he the baby that you thought Denise had—had . . .' she hesitated, wishing she hadn't asked.

But he said quickly, 'No, nothing to do with that episode. Flip came later.' He paused and added a little grimly, 'He was conceived that night she told me she was leaving me for Philip Franklin. I went a little berserk, I'm afraid, although she didn't altogether object.' He laughed harshly. 'I got the story out of her when she asked me to take Flip on. She and Franklin had been lovers for some time—he's loaded, and she fancied his high-flying life-style. But he didn't seem to be suggesting she got a divorce and married him, which was what she wanted. When she found she was pregnant she told him it was his child. He must have had quite a surprise, as he'd had a vasectomy during his first marriage.

'I heard the rest of the story from Franklin himself when I visited him in Paris to check up on Denise's facts,' Rafe went on. 'Apparently he was crazy to get her, but he held back because he couldn't give her any children. After he knew she was going to have a baby, his way was clear and he did the "honourable thing" and asked her to marry him.'

Sara lifted her head. 'Knowing the baby wasn't his?'

'Exactly. It's like a convoluted Hollywood film, isn't it? Wasn't there an old movie called *Whose Baby?*'

Sara said, 'And Flip was born and neither of them told the truth about it? Didn't he—Mr Franklin—mind bringing up another man's son?'

'He's an easy-going type, I don't think he cared much either way. He could afford the best nannies when Flip was little. And, as I said, he was crazy about Denise. It wasn't until just recently, he told me, that the whole thing came out into the open. It's been getting increasingly difficult to cope with Flip when he—Franklin—travelled, and Denise didn't like to let him go off alone—for obvious reasons! So she came up with the idea of passing Flip on to me. She got in touch with my secretary in London and found I was working at the hotel in France, and turned up there with young Flip and her plans all laid. The rest you know.'

Sara sighed. 'We'll give the story a happy ending for Flip, won't we?'

Rafe held her very tightly and his voice was not quite steady as he said, 'I always knew you were a very nice girl, darling Sara.'

She cuddled up against him. 'Not a *very* nice girl, surely? I'm beginning to feel rather shameless just at this moment.'

He caught his breath. 'Is that an invitation, hussy?'

'If you like,' she said meekly.

'I like!' he cried in triumph. He pulled her down on top of him and the magic began all over again.

On an early April evening Alain Savin stood before the entrance to his gallery, where the setting sun was shining through the trees, throwing a rosy glow over the exquisitely engraved crystal entrance door. 'It is very beautiful, and all I had hoped for,' he said with immense pleasure. 'And I have you two good people to thank for it.'

The opening ceremony was just over and the guests had drifted back to the hotel, leaving their host with Rafe and Sara to take a final look at the new gallery.

Seven months had passed since the building had begun, and Rafe and Sara had been married for six of those months. They had travelled backwards and forwards at intervals to oversee the progress of the work, and now, in the spring, they had left Flip in the care of Annette, and come back to be present at the opening ceremony, and at a small party tonight for Alain's closest friends.

'We've enjoyed doing it, haven't we, darling?' Sara slipped her arm through her husband's and smiled up happily into the dark eyes that met hers with such love and pride.

'One of our more successful enterprises,' Rafe agreed, and he glanced across at Alain with a twinkle as he added, 'It's quite surprising how many good things a single contract can lead to.'

'I believe I can guess to what you refer, *mon ami.*' The Frenchman grinned knowingly at the couple before him. 'So—we are all happy, are we not? And when I come here to be in the quiet, among the things I treasure most and all the memories they bring, I shall have another happy memory to add.' He raised Sara's hand gallantly to his lips and met Rafe's eyes with understanding friendship. 'And now I shall leave you here and return to prepare for my little party this evening.'

Rafe and Sara wandered once again through the gallery: down the passage where the new spring green of the trees outside leaned towards the windows, to the big octagonal room at the end. Diffused light fell softly through the glass roof on to Alain's treasures in their niches and cases. Treasures from all around the world, each lovingly arranged to show to best advantage.

Sara paused before a case containing a Japanese kimono. It looked very old, but the lavish flower embroidery still glowed in greens and reds and gold on a deep ivory background. 'I think this is my favourite,' she said. 'A wedding kimono. You always said I was romantic, didn't you?'

'And so you are.' Rafe picked up a strand of her rich red hair and twisted it thoughtfully round her neck. 'Even more now you've finished with being a brunette. I rather like redheads, as you may remember,' he added with a provocative grin.

Sara pulled a face at him. 'Don't remind me!' It was wonderful, now, how they could joke about it. How she could meet Denise occasionally when she visited Flip, and not feel eaten up by jealousy, or bedevilled by lack of confidence. Flip was growing up a bright, happy little boy, and that helped. It was to Sara he turned now, and not his mother. Not that Denise seemed to mind—she lived the life she wanted, and that didn't include a small son.

Sara turned round slowly in the middle of the gallery. 'It's quite amazing—to see your own idea, something you've planned, come into being,' she said in an awed voice. 'Rather like a miracle.'

Rafe nodded and put an arm round her shoulders as they both contemplated the result of their work. 'I know what you mean. And there will be lots more miracles for you, darling.'

They wandered out through the door at the end of the gallery on to the paved piazza beside the lake, where the scent of narcissi hung in the air. Then, by unspoken consent, they turned and walked along to the little wooden gazebo at the end of the narrow line of the shore, and stood looking out over the still water, arms entwined.

'I'll always have a fondness for this place,' Rafe mused. 'This was where I finally came to my senses. Where I found you, and damn near lost you through my own stupidity.'

'Shush!' Sara reached up and covered his mouth. 'Let's just remember the happiness.'

They were silent, each with their own memories. Then Sara said, 'Rafe . . .'

'Hm?' He stroked her hair dreamily.

'You know what you said in there—about there being lots more miracles?'

'Um.'

'Well, I rather think there's going to be another one. A different kind of miracle this time.'

Suddenly he was alert. 'No! You don't mean . . .?' He whirled her round in his arms, staring down into her face, dark eyes glittering. 'When?'

'Around October, probably.' His delight was very sweet to her. 'A good time, don't you think? Annette will be leaving to get married, and Flip will be starting school around then and I'll have a good excuse to be a full-time housewife and mother instead of a part-time one.' A dimple appeared in her cheek. 'I'm getting quite addicted to being a housewife. Not that I've forgotten your promise to make me a partner in the firm one day,' she added hastily.

Rafe took her in his arms and kissed her with such tenderness that the tears sprang into her eyes. 'We're partners already,' he said huskily. 'Partners and lovers—what could be better?'

Sara smiled up into his well-loved face, a face that had finally lost its grim tension and was full of contentment and happy satisfaction. 'I can think of one thing to make it better.' The dimple came into her cheek again. 'Partners, and lovers ... and parents,' she said. 'Agreed?'

He laughed aloud and the sound echoed round the lake. 'Agreed,' he said.

MARCH 1990 HARDBACK TITLES

ROMANCE

A Man Untamed Katherine Arthur	3268	0 263 12379 0
Pulse of the Heartland Melinda Cross	3269	0 263 12380 4
Love at First Sight Sandra Field	3270	0 263 12381 2
The Girl he Left Behind Emma Goldrick	3271	0 263 12382 0
Unspoken Desire Penny Jordan	3272	0 263 12383 9
Dark Pursuit Charlotte Lamb	3273	0 263 12384 7
Man-Trap Marjorie Lewty	3274	0 263 12385 5
A Kiss by Candlelight Joanna Mansell	3275	0 263 12386 3
An Imperfect Love Leigh Michaels	3276	0 263 12387 1
A Christmas Affair Carole Mortimer	3277	0 263 12388 X
A Reckless Loving Joanna Neil	3278	0 263 12389 8
Forbidden Attraction Lilian Peake	3279	0 263 12390 1
Lease on Love Jennifer Taylor	3280	0 263 12391 X
Against all Odds Kay Thorpe	3281	0 263 12392 8
Sea Fever Anne Weale	3282	0 263 12393 6
A Woman's Place Nicola West	3283	0 263 12394 4

MASQUERADE HISTORICAL ROMANCE

Bride for a Rake Una Power	M235	0 263 12491 6
The Diamond Cobra Yvonne Purves	M236	0 263 12492 4

MEDICAL ROMANCE

Surgeon Rivals Margaret Barker	D153	0 263 12489 4
Vets at Variance Mary Bowring	D154	0 263 12490 8

LARGE PRINT

A Matter of Will Robyn Donald	311	0 263 12343 X
Love's Fugitive Rachel Ford	312	0 263 12344 8
Come Back to Me Catherine George	313	0 263 12345 6
Seductive Stranger Charlotte Lamb	314	0 263 12346 4
Love is for the Lucky Susanne McCarthy	315	0 263 12347 2
Riddell of Rivermoon Miriam Macgregor	316	0 263 12348 0
Island Turmoil Annabel Murray	317	0 263 12349 9
Wish for the Moon Sally Wentworth	318	0 263 12350 2

Mills & Boon

APRIL 1990 HARDBACK TITLES

ROMANCE

Title	Author	No.	ISBN
Shattered Trust	Jacqueline Baird	3284	0 263 12399 5
The Tiger's Lair	Helen Bianchin	3285	0 263 12400 2
Echoes in the Night	Rosemary Carter	3286	0 263 12401 0
Love's Awakening	Rachel Ford	3287	0 263 12402 9
The Music of Love	Kay Gregory	3288	0 263 12403 7
Passionate Awakening	Diana Hamilton	3289	0 263 12404 5
Bride of Ravenscroft	Sally Heywood	3290	0 263 12405 3
An Adult Love	Sarah Holland	3291	0 263 12406 1
An Impossible Passion	Stephanie Howard	3292	0 263 12407 X
Breaking Away	Penny Jordan	3293	0 263 12408 8
Spellbinding	Charlotte Lamb	3294	0 263 12409 6
It All Depends on Love	Roberta Leigh	3295	0 263 12410 X
The Girl with Green Eyes	Betty Neels	3296	0 263 12411 8
Wild Flower Wind	Morgan Patterson	3297	0 263 12412 6
The Loving Touch	Catherine Spencer	3298	0 263 12413 4
The Golden Thief	Kate Walker	3299	0 263 12414 2

MASQUERADE HISTORICAL ROMANCE

Title	Author	No.	ISBN
Honour Bound	Helen Dickson	M237	0 263 12535 1
A Most Unsuitable Duchess	Gail Mallin	M238	0 263 12536 X

MEDICAL ROMANCE

Title	Author	No.	ISBN
Repentant Angel	Lynne Collins	D155	0 263 12533 5
A Medical Liaison	Sharon Wirdnam	D156	0 263 12534 3

LARGE PRINT

Title	Author	No.	ISBN
The Marrying Game	Lindsay Armstrong	319	0 263 12351 0
Goodbye Forever	Sandra Field	320	0 263 12352 9
So Close and no Closer	Penny Jordan	321	0 263 12353 7
A Special Arrangement	Madeleine Ker	322	0 263 12354 5
With no Reservations	Leigh Michaels	323	0 263 12355 3
Frozen Enchantment	Jessica Steele	324	0 263 12356 1
Leap in the Dark	Kate Walker	325	0 263 12357 X
The Chain of Destiny	Betty Neels	326	0 263 12358 8

4 Mills & Boon Paperbacks can be yours absolutely FREE.

Enjoy a wonderful world of Romance....

Passionate and intriguing, sensual and exciting. A top quality selection of four Mills & Boon titles written by leading authors of Romantic Fiction can be delivered direct to your door absolutely **FREE**.

Try these Four Free books as your introduction to Mills & Boon Reader Service. You can be among the thousands of women who enjoy brand new Romances every month **PLUS** a whole range of special benefits.

THE NEWEST PAPERBACK ROMANCES —
reserved at the printers for you each month and delivered direct to you by Mills & Boon — POSTAGE & PACKING FREE.

FREE MONTHLY NEWSLETTER
packed with exciting competitions, horoscopes, recipes and handicrafts PLUS information on top Mills & Boon authors.

SPECIAL OFFERS
Specially selected books and bargain gifts created just for Mills & Boon subscribers.

There is no commitment whatsoever, no hidden extra charges and your first parcel of four books is absolutely free.

Why not send for details now? Simply write to Mills & Boon Reader Service, Dept HBEP, P.O. Box 236, Thornton Road, Croydon, Surrey CR9 3RU, or telephone our helpful, friendly girls at Mills & Boon on 01-684 2141 and we will send you details about the Mills & Boon Reader Service Subscription Scheme.

You'll soon be able to join us in a wonderful world of Romance!

Please note: Readers in South Africa write to:
Independent Book Services Pty
Postbag X3010, Randburg 2125, S. Africa.